COLLECT...

FICTION

To Lizzy

Signed with love

[signature]

Chiado Publishing
chiadopublishing.com

All characters and events in this publication, other than those clearly in the public domain, are ficticious and any resemblance to real persons, living or dead, is purely coincidential.

chiadopublishing.com

U.K | U.S.A | Ireland
Kemp House
152 City Road
London
EC1CV 2NX

Spain
Calle Gran Via
71 - 2.ª planta
28013 Madrid
España

France | Belgium | Luxembourg
Porte de Paris
50 Avenue du President Wilson
Bâtiment 112
La Plaine St Denis 93214
France

Germany
Kurfürstendamm 21
10719 Berlin
Deutschland

Portugal | Brazil | Angola | Cape Verde
Avenida da Liberdade
Nº 166, 1º Andar
1250-166 Lisboa
Portugal

Copyright © 2013 by Chiado Publishing and Chris Brown
All rights reserved.

Web: www.chiadopublishing.com | www.chiadoglobal.com

Title: One Man to Love, One Man to Live
Author: Chris Brown

Graphic Design Ps_design – Departamento Gráfico

Printed and Bound by: *Chiado Print*

ISBN: 978-989-51-0468-0
Legal Deposit n.º 360280/13

CHRIS BROWN

ONE MAN TO LOVE ONE MAN TO LIVE

Chiado Publishing

Crystal woke on the chimes of seven am, adjusted her eyes to the light already breaking through the curtains and felt a heavy weight sink in her heart. Next to her lay the man she loved, in her bed, under her roof and yet it didn't seem like heaven. If she could dream a genie to wish her a man with all the physical traits she wished for, then he would be perfect. The only trouble was, his mind was as empty as the dustbin that had just been collected outside. The sex was amazing, but the pillow talk was already asleep before it got started. Conversation in Crystal's world consisted of her voice and the occasional returned grunt, something she was going to have to do something about.

Crystal started to get out of bed and adjusted her slip when a hand grabbed at her waist and pulled her back in. There was no mistaking what lay ahead in the next twenty five minutes. Maybe there would be a little heavy petting or a little sucking on the left breast perhaps. Always the left! Then would follow some sweat inducing hard fuck that would rid her perfect man of his morning erection. There was nothing especially bad about the whole affair, except maybe the right nipple could see some affection, more a matter of same old, same old.

Now she would need a shower before dressing and already the day was following the same steady rituals. What would follow would be the dash to dress, the dash for the train and a finger crossing hope to be at work before the boss. Crystal almost prayed now for that genie, if only to wish for something a little different.

Crystal sat on the train, courtesy of a seat given up by a slightly balding, slightly podgy business man. She was convinced his noble deed was so that a view down her cleavage could be seen from his now standing position. His constant averting gaze confirmed she was probably right. Whilst his peering made Crystal somewhat uncomfortable, she couldn't help but wonder if he was a left or right nipple man!

Two stops down and the businessman departed with the question unasked. It was probably better she didn't know Crystal thought. The carriage was starting to get less crowded now and attentions were being drawn to that of there being just one more stop before she too would have to depart and take the short walk to the office. There has to be more to life than this.

The events that were to follow were to change life for Crystal forever. If there was a wish made to an unseen genie, then he certainly heard and came good, and it all started with that short walk to work.

One thousand, seven hundred and forty three steps, one flight of stairs, two changes in direction, crossing one road. The exact walk from the train to the office, of course assuming the lure of chocolate from the newsagents hadn't gripped. Today that lure was to be the catalyst to all of the changes that would become Crystal's life.

He was there, still slightly bald and still slightly podgy. It was if she had been given another chance to ask the question that plagued her thoughts only minutes previous. Crystal smiled and their gazes met, all the time in her head she could hear 'lefty or righty' over and over. And so she asked. She came straight out with it in the middle of the newsagents. 'Do you prefer to suck on the left or right nipple?'

As the realisation of what she'd just said sank in, and seemingly endless wait for the sort of reply she expected ticked on, it was with admiration and a new found appreciation that saw Crystal hanging on every word of her questioned gentleman's answer.

'Whilst I would happily die a thousand deaths in the bountiful bosom of which you have been bestowed, seeing to the needs of both left and right, it is first the mind of the woman that would ask such a question I would first wish to tend."

It was definitely a far cry from the 'I'd suck on both those fun bags!' Crystal was expecting.

His name was Sean, somewhat more advanced in years than Crystal but softly spoken and considerate. There was nothing about his physical demeanour that she found attractive and yet there was an acceptance of a meeting for coffee and a spot of lunch. It must have been the manner in which he spoke and more importantly listened within that brief encounter that left her wanting more.

The hours leading to lunch seemed to drag like a Monday morning after a heavy weekend. All Crystal could think about was reengaging in conversation with Sean about life, the universe and his cradling of her bountiful bosom. The lingering thought of the latter was inducing a fluttering effect within Crystal's stomach and she couldn't pin point why, especially considering her earlier fuck that morning with her dream bodied man.

Lunchtime had never arrived with such a mix of conflicting emotions. On the one hand, butterflies were fluttering within Crystal's stomach like those of a love struck teen having received a kiss off her one true love. On the other, the realisation that she was about to meet a complete stranger of whom she had asked about sucking her nipples. If she really had wished for 'more than this' then that's exactly what she was getting.

Sean was already there as Crystal arrived at their agreed lunch spot. As she walked up to him, she was in awe to see him rise from his seat and wait patiently for her to be seated before returning to his. Such a gentleman, but she'd already come to that conclusion earlier in the day. Crystal was aware that something had changed in him since that impromptu meeting this morning. Gone was the conception of a balding, podgy letch. Now sat before her was a sincere, trusting man who eyes bore holes into her soul like the sun through a magnifying glass. And upon every word he spoke she again hung. Conversation ebbed and flowed, likes and dislikes ambitions and regrets. To every question came a near perfect response. Similarities across all aspects of life were to be found. It was as if the more they talked the more Crystal felt like her mind was being subjected to a form of foreplay. The more common ground they found, the more she was being aroused by this man she'd only just begun to know.

Crystal stood, catching Sean unawares he rose a second or two later. Making her excuses, she hastily made her way to the bathroom. She needed a few moments of composure, to reassure herself that what was happening was just a platonic meeting of minds.

Crystal made her way back to the table, and again Sean stood and waited upon her taking her seat. During her absence the food had arrived and so with exchanged smiles, they both engaged in picking from the platter they had ordered. As conversation continued to flow, it was now the little things Crystal begun to notice. He didn't speak with his mouth full, nor eat with his mouth open. He used a napkin to wipe and would always pick from the plate once she had. If this was some front in order to impress, then Sean was certainly a master of the art.

Ten to one arrived all too soon, and what had been a wonderful lunch date was coming to an end. Sean enquired about the possibility of meeting again, however much to Crystal's amazement he had neither mobile phone, nor social network contact. All they had was an agreement to meet again in the same place, at the same time a week from today. For the first time since they had met in the newsagents earlier that morning, Crystal couldn't help but feel a little disappointed.

All afternoon she could not rid him from her thoughts. He was perfect in all ways except from the fact she didn't find him attractive. Was she being fickle in not being able to look past the physical appearance, when he made her feel so alive in all other aspects? More importantly, she already had the most perfect bodied man waiting for her at home, which meant her actions at lunch was tantamount to cheating. Crystal pondered on whether it was actually a thing, Mind Cheating. Real or not, Crystal had no intention of stopping, in fact she'd only just begun.

Crystal left work for the day and made her way to the station. Rain started to fall and yet it was unable to dampen her high spirits. She couldn't help but wonder if Sean would be on the return train home due to the fact he was on her train that morning. The entire journey and despite eagerly scanning each platform they stopped, there was no sign of Sean. Despite this, Crystal's mood was high. She traced his name on the window whilst outside the rain fell heavier. It was going to be horrible last section of her journey, but it seemed to go unnoticed.

Crystal got off the train and made the walk back home in torrential rain. She was soaked to the bone by the time the sanctuary of her home was found. The central heating was a comforting invisible hug that greeted her. At the point of removing her coat and gloves, her man appeared. He was dressed in just a pair of boxers he had clearly preempted her arrival home from work. Layer by layer Crystal stripped from her rain soaked clothes until she stood totally naked. Despite the warmth around her, Crystal shivered. There was passion there in the hall way, and up the stairs to the bedroom. The two locked in an embrace that both penetrated and unified their lust for each other. He grabbed at her wet bedraggled hair whilst a mixture kissing, licking and sucking removed the last traces of rain from her body. Crystal threw her head back as climax was reached, sadly however not by her. They both laid on the bed in silence in a game of 'who's going to move first?'

Today had been an almost perfect day. Two separate fuck sessions with her lover and the most memorable encounter with a man with whom touched her mind like no other. Crystal smiled to herself and thanked the genie who had obviously heard her thoughts that morning. Life was changing and for the first time in a long time, Crystal was enjoying the change. If only she didn't have to now prepare tea and return to the mundane household chores, the almost perfect would be perfect.

Crystal knew that she adored her man. What she'd been asking herself the last several months of their relationship was did she actually love her man, or his perfectly formed fat free hairless smooth, yet firm, body. Not to mention the seven inches he gave to her at almost every occasion, because oh my god, that was enough of a band aid to cover any wounds in the relationship. The steady realisation that maybe she had become somewhat shallow as a person was beginning to dawn.

The next few days withdraw back to the normal mundane routine Crystal had become so accustomed. There had been no sightings of Sean on any of the trains, either to work or home and with no way to contact him, it was just a matter of counting the days until their agreed date. He had begun to plague her mind to the point of obsession. Despite the flowing conversation that day over lunch, Crystal was still unaware of Sean's career, whether he was in a relationship or even married. The latter sent a cold shiver down her spine, but for reasons unexplainable. Why did it matter if he was married? Crystal herself was already in a relationship and yet the thought of Sean being unavailable suddenly filled her with sadness.

Sunday, Crystal's favourite day of the week had arrived. She was awoken from her slumber by her man's head buried between her legs working her with both this fingers and tongue. Upon realising Crystal had awoken he proceeded to kiss a trail from where he started, across her stomach to her left breast. Crystal sighed as he played with her nipple, ninety percent out of pleasure, and the other ten out of the monotony of it all. Lifting her hips to assist her lover's attempts to seek penetration, Crystal groaned as the full weight of his lust bore down on her. Several times he took her to edge of eternal bliss, and several times he shifting her position to prevent it being reached. She adored the way he could manipulate her to his will, putting her in positions to stimulate themselves further. They reached climax simultaneously and together slumped in sweaty heaps on the bed. This was why Crystal loved Sundays.

The other good thing about Sundays was the solitude and peacefulness. Shortly her man would shower and dress, head to the gym for an hour or so, then run around a field kicking a ball about for two hours to finally round out the day down the pub with his mates drinking to either celebrate or commiserate. In the meantime Crystal knew the washing and ironing pile would need attending to at some point and if she was lucky would find a little time before preparing tea to sit and indulge in her most prized pastime, reading. If she was able to escape reality for just a couple of hours within the pages of a good book, then having to attend to the chores was a small sacrifice to pay. It was yet another ritual Crystal had become accustomed to over their years together.

The thing about rituals routines or life timetables, whatever you wish to call them, is that although they organise the day to day tedium into an efficient machine, it can also put the wheels into a soggy rut difficult to get out of. Sean arrived at a time in Crystal's life when a tow truck was being pondered. He was a little piece of haphazard in her normal predictability.

Crystal woke early, even for a Monday. She placed her hand in her man's groin and started to awaken him with slow firm rubs. Such was the desire burning within her, as soon as signs of life were beginning to show she straddled across him and began to tease herself. Being in full control Crystal varied the intensity and depth in which she rode upon him. This was clearly for her pleasure and hers alone. The end result was an orgasm that was as intense as any she'd experienced and left her in a state of numbness below the waist. As way of reward for being the dutiful boyfriend and allowing her to do as she pleased, she took him in her mouth and allowed him to reach a climax of his own. A shower was now definitely needed.

The day was starting very well indeed and if only the rest of it could follow in similar fashion then Crystal would be a happy bunny indeed. She had always been of the opinion that if you start the week in a positive frame of mind, then you're better placed mentally to tackle the daily problems ahead, or more up for the challenge of finding someone to offload them onto. Today was going to be good, as tomorrow was going to be better. Tomorrow was the day she was meeting back up with Sean.

No day for as long as Crystal could remember had arrived with such anticipation on its lead up, and childish glee upon its arrival. The outfit she was to wear had been arranged the night before, provocative, yet still professional for work. The last thing Crystal wanted was to be the focus of the office gossip, not again. Whilst pulling on some rather eye catching stockings a familiar hand made a play for her attention. It pulled her closer as kisses tenderly played their way across her lower back. And for the first time in their relationship, Crystal pulled away. There was a grunt as the duvet devoured all remnants of beautiful naked man that lay next to her. Excuses of needing to be in early fell on deaf ears as she continued to dress. There was going to have to be some good make-up sex on the agenda this evening.

The train journey into work was one that tormented Crystal. Sean had not been there as she had very much hoped, and guilt wracked her mind at having refused her man's advances. 'Why didn't I fuck him?' she muttered. 'He has the most perfect cock and yet still I didn't fuck him.' The torment was an annoying distraction to what should have been a most wonderful day.

It was at the next stop Crystal was aware of an elderly woman eyeing her disapprovingly whilst waiting to leave the train. 'Dressed like that my dear, I'm surprised you didn't fuck him either' and with that she made her way onto the platform. Two horrifying moments of realisation smacked Crystal like a heavy weight boxer. Firstly, the slit in her dress was clearly allowing too much flesh and stocking to be seen by all and sundry. The second, her muttering had been loud enough to have been heard by the other passengers. Crystal called out after the old woman 'I will fuck him tonight though!' but she had already gone. Unlike the rest of the passengers now intent on staring as Crystal fought with her skirt.

The time taken to navigate the remaining two stops was such, that there was a possibility the slow boat to China would have reached its destination first. When the train finally arrived, Crystal stood to a small ripple of applause from some college lads towards the back of the carriage. Flattered by the compliment, she blew a kiss in their general direction. For a woman whose life was ruled by routine and ritual, to the point of having counted every step from train to office door during a morning of boredom, Tuesdays were becoming quite whimsical.

Lunchtime couldn't come soon enough. Today the life in real estate was no more exciting than the view from the window. Crystal cursed at her hurried attempt to get into work and her missing out on the bar of chocolate that would have helped with the tediousness. Instead she turned her mind to all the questions she would ask Sean when they met again in a few hours. The clock on the wall teased her with a tick that seemed strangely louder and slower than normal. Even the office gossip rounds did nothing to bring the elusive twelve o'clock closer, although a consolation was that Crystal didn't feature in them. Well, at least to her knowledge.

Crystal was already halfway out the door as lunch arrived. Ignoring the questions from colleagues about the speed of her departure, she made her way to the eatery where she just knew Sean would be waiting. He didn't disappoint. There were flashes of déjà vu as Sean stood upon Crystal's approach offering her again a seat before taking his and it wasn't long before the two of them found themselves lost in conversation. So easy was their chatting that all the questions Crystal had planned tumbled out of her mouth in a verbal barrage that seemed to leave Sean dumbfounded. For the first time he seemed to scramble for answers as if looking for the ones he thought Crystal would want to hear.

Sean held his head in his hands and Crystal couldn't help but fear the little bubble of happiness she'd built up around this blossoming friendship was about to burst. More questions raced around her already spinning confused mind, but she refrained from asking these out loud. Nothing could have prepared her for what she was about to discover though, as Sean answered her questions with an almost a sense of shame in his honesty.

He was poor. The reason for not being on the train home was because he had spent the last of his money on the lunch they shared and so walked that evening. A struggling writer, he would come into the city once a week in an attempt to sell his work to whoever may be interested. He wasn't married, nor was he seeing anyone. His writing was his mistress and consumed most of his waking hours despite selling only a handful of pieces. As the confessions flowed forth in Sean's frank and open life story, the only part to have resonated within Crystal's thought process was the fact he was single. Her little bubble was intact and growing.

Crystal reassured Sean that all he had said hadn't shown him in an unfavourable light. Much to the contrary, she respected his honesty and the kindness he had shown paying for a meal he could hardly afford. She moved her chair a little closer in a gesture that the friendship was still very much alive. It would also ensure Sean would get a view similar to that shown to her fellow commuters this morning.

One o'clock arrived and went. Crystal could not wait another week again for just an hour spent in the company of someone who knew how to hold a conversation and treated her with respect. Ignoring that was the frequent wayward glance towards her leg and stockings, because she had put it on a plate. A quick phone call to the office with the complaint of an on setting migraine, and she was suddenly free to spend the remainder of the afternoon in Sean's company.

Conversation returned to its free flowing state with clarifications of discussions they'd had in their first meeting re-visited as well as Sean's confessions during this talked of. Crystal herself offered of herself tales about her career and her feelings of monotony in her day to day life, and yet when asked of any romantic connections a denial toppled off her tongue as easy as if it had been true. For the second time in a day, Crystal felt herself consumed by guilt. She was sat with a man that did nothing for her physically, and yet having spurned her own man's advances this morning was now showing this guy more leg than any high end hooker. Crystal tried to dismiss the idea of actually being sexually aroused by Sean with the very notion of being turned on by mere words as comical. That was until the recollection of what she'd done in restroom only last week added a weight of realism to her thoughts. Conversation was hastily turned to Sean's writing.

Sean was a short fiction writer, setting his tales in the romance, grime and gothic notion of many people's idea of Victorian London. Sadly, many others aspiring to seek fame in fortune in literary world have pitched their stake in this genre making knock backs more frequent than acceptance. Crystal enquired about the reading of any such tales Sean had written, and duly he responded by handing over a small leather bound book. There was no doubting its age due to the way the leather was worn and cracked and inside pages literally spilled forth words, sentences and entire paragraphs of ideas and inspiration. Crystal thumbed each page with a desire resembling that of a small child receiving a much wanted gift. Each word was read and reread, every line consumed into her open and embracing mind. Yet again she found herself being stimulated by this man's words, almost aroused by tripping through the thought processes and imagination of this person before her.

Crystal had become so sidetracked with reading, she was oblivious to the fact Sean was sat quietly writing. A curiosity compelled her to ask of his current work and if she could herself read it. The word 'no' didn't appear to be within Sean's vocabulary as he handed over the sheet of paper. Crystal read,

'I was travelling to London by way of public carriage on a matter of business. The journey was tedious for the most part, stopping occasionally to rejuvenate the numbers. It was upon one such stop that a female joined our company. I moved myself accordingly to allow her comfortable seating upon which courteous smiles were exchanged. I could not help but notice her attire was akin to that of a madam, but yet she presented herself with class and dignity. It was true also that my gaze may have perhaps noticed her heaving bosom, to which may have wandered my mind to the gutter. Regrettably we did not share in each other's company long as my travels end came before hers, much the pity.'

The inevitable smile loomed large across Crystal's face upon finishing. She had gone to hand it back when Sean gestured for her to keep it. Whilst it didn't seem possible, her smile grew.

The afternoon was drawing to a close when Sean made his apologies about having to leave. He had an arranged meeting about a small article in a literary paper. They stood together gathering their belongings, and discussed when they would next meet. It was then Sean leaned in towards Crystal and she instinctively closed her eyes at the expectation of contact. Instead he quietly whispered in her ear, 'Never be afraid to chase your dreams poor, over never dreaming rich. Until next week my muse.' By the time Crystal had opened her eyes, Sean was heading for the door. He briefly looked back with a smile and was soon gone. A heavy sigh drifted from Crystal's lip, 'Seven fucking days!'

The entire journey home Crystal thumbed at the writing Sean had given here. Her thoughts were mulling over the idea he thought she looked like a sophisticated hooker, trying to recollect which low neckline top she had been wearing when they first met. Her own glance caught sight of the high slit in her skirt and her stockings on show as flash backs of the morning's journey made her laugh a little too loud. However, something else played on Crystal's mind. Had she just allowed Sean to pay for yet another lunch having been told previously the last time he walked home? Today was a day for guilt.

Crystal returned home to the unusual sound of raised male voices coming from the living room. There was no mistaking though, the infernal racket coming from her boyfriend's games console. This was no doubt her punishment for shunning sex this morning, so a bath by candle light and a good book seemed an appealing alternative to suffering the male company. Upon entering the kitchen it was strewn with empty beer cans and take-away wrappers. Crystal opted against announcing her home coming, instead took herself upstairs for her bath.

In a state of shock and confusion, Crystal woke naked on the bed. Her boyfriend stood next to her in a similar state of undress. He was erect and most eager. When the reality of the situation dawned on her, Crystal sat up and took her man in her mouth. She started going through all the little things she knew he liked. Teasing him with her tongue and stoking slowly with her hands. It was then Crystal sensed they weren't alone. A noise from the corner alerted her to a figure watching them, one whose silhouette was eerily familiar. As she strained to see who it was, she found her thrown backwards onto the bed. Crystal let out a groan as her man entered her and proceeded to satisfy his own primal urges. There was no passion, no foreplay, just pure unadulterated sex. By now the shadowy figure had approached the bed and through ecstasy filled eyes Crystal could see it was Sean.

A bump and a clatter woke Crystal again. This time she was in the bath and the water had started to turn cold. Getting out and reaching for a towel there was a degree of relief flooding over her at the realisation that the previous events had been but a dream. Upon entering the bedroom, it also became evident that the noise that woke her was that of her drunken boyfriend falling into bed. He lay there fully clothed, sound asleep and snoring. After throwing on some comfy clothes, Crystal closed the door and made her way downstairs to start tidying up.

The following morning arrived to the sound of aches and groans. Crystal's were from the fact she had fallen asleep on the sofa whilst reading a book. It was not the most comfortable of nights sleep and she was paying for it now. Those coming from upstairs were the self-inflicted, too much alcohol the night before kind. Sex was definitely off the agenda this morning. If it were not for the fact she had taken the afternoon off yesterday, work would have been too. Reluctantly Crystal dressed and readied herself for another day in the office. Today would be a good day to detour for some chocolate.

The thing about taking impromptu time off work is that when you return it inevitably means explaining yourself to the boss. Crystal had a love hate relationship with hers. For the most part she loved working for him, and was grateful for the opportunities open to her in such a high paid job. However selling real estate was his life and that is where the hate came in. He expected his staff to live and breathe it too, so bunking an afternoon was not going to go down well. Crystal braced herself for the worst, but yet it never came. Instead of being disciplined, she was actually being praised for her work and dedication over the past few months. Furthermore, there was to an internal promotion and she was to be considered a candidate for the role. 'Any minute now I'm going to wake up on the bloody train aren't I?' rolled from Crystal's lips just a little too loud. Her boss smiled and dismissed her back to her duties stating a decision would be made within a couple of weeks.

Ordinarily, more precisely before meeting Sean, Crystal would have been ecstatic at being up for promotion. It could be the exact thing she had been wishing on that gene for, something to change the monotony that had become her life. Whilst real estate wasn't the most glamorous of careers, it had afforded her a lifestyle she had come to live up to. In fact, there were times when she thought only money could have snagged her the man she had, but to come home to that body the price was worth it. And yet the words whispered in her ear only yesterday sat on her conscience like a devil in a cartoon. Though Crystal couldn't remember the exact words, she knew it meant the seeking of dreams rather than giving up on them to be rich.

The more the day went on, it became obvious that there were a couple of other drawbacks to being absent without leave. Firstly, no body picks up your work and so your to-do-list looks like it would struggle to fit on an economy roll of toilet paper. Secondly, you become today's focus for the gossip mongers and office whisperers. Crystal always believed that gossip was a good way of finding out things about yourself you didn't already know. Proof being, that when she thought yesterdays sultry skirt and suspenders had gone un-noticed, there were the comments to shatter the illusion. Whether it was the chocolate, the talk of promotion or the fact she still ached all over, Crystal somehow managed to brush it aside with a smile and bury her head into her work.

The remainder of the working hours passed without too many dramas. There was the occasional jibe during lunch about not having somewhere or *someone* to run off to today, but for the most part it was very much a case of 'same shit, different day.' Type a few Emails, arrange a few meetings and take phone calls, a lot of phone calls. Crystal once totalled the number of hours in the working day she had spent with a phone to her ear. Of the seven hours spent at her desk the amount was close to five. That was almost three hundred minutes of each working day spent talking to people. Not a bad way to make good money. It was probably why all she wanted when she got home was mind blowing sex.

The good thing about having a busy day is that it prevents the mind from churning through things on one's mind. Sadly the return journey home brought them crashing back like a thundering herd of wilder beast. All the way home Crystal juggled the notion of a promotion against chasing her dreams, being rich and being poor. However there was dirt in the gears that stopped them turning smoothly, prevented the dilemma being brought to a sensible resolution. 'What dreams have I worth chasing?'

Crystal's mind began to wander through her childhood, hoping to find the dreams she once had. Aged four, maybe five, full of the innocence of youth dreams where to be a fairy princess with wings, tiara and magic wand. An ideal aspiration for a woman rapidly closing in on thirty she thought. In her pre-teen years all Crystal wanted was bigger boobs, longer legs and for boys to notice her amongst the crowd. Neatly packed in with the invisible kids, Crystal dreamed of being one of the popular girls. A smile graced her at the acknowledgement of those particular dreams having come true. Early twenties and it was all about independence and money. Having had several jobs and enjoying perhaps too much of an active social life, these dreams had well and truly been conquered. Crystal's thoughts brought her to her late twenties and bang up to date. The only dreams she could think to chase now, were to defy the effects gravity was having on her body and then find an adult sized fairy princess costume.

Crystal's mind continued to wander to childhood friends and those social weekends spent with 'the girls' partying to excess. All the alcohol, all the men and the total regret on Monday mornings. How had she allowed those times to just drift away? Had she really become so entwined with her work and her man to have forgotten she once had another life? And what of her friends, had they all managed to chase their dreams or where they still living the lives they all once shared. A catch up was definitely needed, as was getting off the train before her day dreaming made her miss another stop.

A walk that should have taken just ten minutes had now become a forty five minute magical mystery tour. Crystal was adamant in her mind that Sean was going to get the blame for this. If not for those words softly spoken, then there would have been no day dreaming, no missed stop and routines would have been kept. A contradicting thought dared to challenge proceedings by highlighting her own desire to break free from her own daily rituals, the very same desires that introduced her to Sean in the first place. Crystal let out a scream into the otherwise silent early evening air, then proceeded to apologise to every face that appeared at twitching curtains.

By the time Crystal finally arrived home she was aching more than she was this morning. Her feet were throbbing, her head was pounding and her back felt worse than it had all day. All she wanted was to kick off her shoes and fall into bed. In reality she was going to have to cook a meal, clean the dishes and prepare an outfit for tomorrow before the luxury of bed could be considered. Crystal was all too aware of the short comings dating a man who was still clinging desperately to his youth, but wished just once for the boy to play out while the man stay home. As expected, he was sat watching sport on the TV with a beer in hand. He turned and smiled as Crystal appeared in the doorway to which her heart melted like ice in the sun. Smiling back she went to prepare the tea her aches and pains a distant memory.

Meal times were usually a quiet affair, even more so when there was football on. As much as Crystal tried to engage her man in conversation about her day very little seemed to register. Even when she attempted to discuss the finer aspects of the beautiful game, it was met with dampened enthusiasm. The fact she didn't know her Rovers from her Uniteds may have been a defining reason. It was for these reasons the possibility of a promotion at work went un-discussed, not to mention her meetings with Sean. 'I'm inviting a couple of the girls round later and we're going to dress up for you in naughty underwear' Crystal playfully suggested. The prolonged silence just emphasized the point further.

With chores done, Crystal made her way to the bedroom. The sound of running could be heard behind her, and so she too hastened her speed before flinging herself on the bed. She was joined by a man whose hangover that morning had either disappeared or was being suppressed by that evening's drinking. What was blatantly obvious also was that he was feeling incredibly horny. Straddling himself across her, he proceeded to work his magic in making clothes just disappear. He also possessed the magic touch when it came to finding 'that' spot. Crystal groaned and squirmed as he brought her to climax. She pleaded with him to take her as her turned his attention to the left breast. She dragged her nails down his back when finally he obliged and gave to her all of himself. It wasn't long before they both lay on the bed in a sweaty satisfied state.

Sleep would not come to Crystal as it had her man. Instead she lay on the bed with thoughts of the past fortnight coursing through her mind. She turned and stared at the man lying next to her. In her heart she knew she loved him, not just for his amazingly defined well proportioned body, but because every time her eyes met his, the butterflies fluttered within her stomach as they did when they first met. Was he marriage material? Did he love her as she loved him? Would he follow her to the ends of the Earth? There were no answers to these questions. What of Sean? Crystal knew for fact there was no sexual attraction, but yet she could not stop her inbuilt instinct to appeal to that which all men succumb, flirtation. Sean stimulated her in a way her man couldn't and the past two weeks had shown her she needed this in her life. Was there room for both? While for now it seemed there was, but what if she did indeed get the promotion? Was there going to be room for either of them?

The sound of the alarm woke Crystal from what seemed only a few minutes of sleep. She nudged herself up against her man in the hope that he would help to wake her from her weary state. He didn't disappoint, almost rolling on top he started to kiss all down her back whilst with his hand he caressed the curves of her lower cheeks. Crystal groaned at the pleasurable sensations, and then a little more when she felt the excited state of her man pushing to where his hands had been. She lifted herself onto all fours as the unmistakable feeling of her man entering her erased all of her remaining weariness. He gripped her by the hips and pounded away as if his life depended upon it. After what seemed like more time than she had been asleep, her man reached his crescendo just as Crystal was reaching hers. She waited for him to slump back on the bed and then headed for the shower, pausing briefly to look back and declare 'I love you' in sultry fashion. There was an acknowledgement of sorts as he pulled at the duvet to cover his naked body.

Work attire for today was a little more subdued. Not liking very much being the centre of gossip over the wearing of stockings under a high slit skirt, trousers and blouse was today's choice. Before Crystal had had a chance to fully dress, there came a snoring from under the duvet. 'Bless him' she thought leaving the bedroom to finish getting ready. Friday's were easy days filled with end of week meetings and report type ups. Throw in an above average number of tea breaks and with any luck she would be home drama free and it would still feel like the same day. Of course now having dared to think that way, it was all going to do opposite and become the day from Hell. 'Oh well I've been fucked already, let's see if the day wants to fuck me too'. The omens weren't good as the heavens opened halfway in getting to the station.

By the time the train had reached Crystal's stop the rain had subsided to a light drizzle. 'Perhaps the day might not be so bad after all' she thought out loud, and for the most part she was right. The rumour mill was in full force as allegedly Jenny in accounts was caught doing the dirty with one of the directors, and if previous gossip was true, she certainly likes to share it around the workforce. Rumour has it, Marie-Anne from human resources left after being caught with her in a similar predicament. It was no wonder Jenny always had a pleasant demeanour about her all day.

Jenny had everything Crystal envied in a woman. She was lively and bubbly with youthful exuberance. Being a size ten at most with cute firm breasts and perky nipples, that was often evident on summer days through figure hugging clothes. Her arse didn't look like it would block out the sun if she bent over either, and of course she didn't mind which side her bread was buttered. Not that Crystal had ever considered batting for the other team, but having the freedom of choice was somewhat enviable. She was certainly the poster girl for the company and many a man's, and women's, ideal fuck.

Lunchtime arrived and Crystal decided to take a walk and maybe even treat herself a little. As she reached for the door another truth of the office rumour mill hit home. Even if you are not the focus of today's gossip, it takes longer than a couple of days for them to forget past misdemeanours. Crystal left with the taunts fading behind the closing door and headed to that which every woman needed in her life, apart from chocolate, designer clothes and pretty shoes. As she wandered the aisles looking at everything longingly she recalled how an ex lover had showered her with such finery on a regular basis. He had claimed 'She was a gift to him from the Gods, and as such he would afford her the very best so that he may unwrap her again and again.' Crystal also recalled how the half dozen maxed out credit cards had led their break up.

With that in mind Crystal put down the very expensive but very lovely shoes she had been admiring. Perhaps if she was to get the promotion then these could be her treat to herself. Time then for literary therapy and a trip to a little second hand book shop she liked to frequent. Inside was small dark and dreary with books rammed into the bookshelves making it almost impossible for anyone to remove them. It was indeed a plethora or indeed cornucopia of dedication to the written word. An old armchair sat in a tiny clutter free area so that customers could sit and read, though they seldom did. This was not a shop intent on making millions from the sheep of society, but of love and devotion. To clinging on to a history technology was intent on replacing. High end fashion to scruffy second hand books, such were the things that made Crystal happy.

With two new romantic novels bought for the comparable cost of half a heel on one of shoes she had promised herself earlier, Crystal made her way to the bookshop door. Impulse, curiosity or even divine intervention stopped her in her tracks. She searched in her handbag for the now crumpled up piece of paper with the words Sean had written for her. Returning to the owner of the shop, she put it under his nose, 'Doesn't this sound like it could be a thoroughly interesting read?' The owner read slowly and upon finishing agreed that it would, if there was more of it. 'Would you sell it if there was more?' Crystal enquired enthusiastically. 'My dear, if it's a book, then I'll sell it.' Thanking him again, she returned the piece of paper to her bag and left the shop with a broad smile. Now all she had to do was convince Sean to finish what he started.

Crystal headed back to work in high spirits and was feeling very pleased with herself. Her mood however, was dampened by that of the office upon her return. Waiting for her on her desk was an internal memo which stated next Friday was employee appraisals, attendance by all staff mandatory. It was no wonder the mood was sombre. In her absence she had been nominated by her delightful colleagues as the first 'victim', something they found highly amusing. Crystal knew the last laugh was hers having already been praised for her work the day before.

As the afternoon passed and the working week came to a close, it was becoming increasingly evident that only one other seemed to take the news of appraisals in her stride, Jenny. She was still being as bubbly as ever without a care in the world. Crystal couldn't help but wonder if she was being appraised at the time of being caught. For a moment she envied the person that found them, saw her in the flesh. Crystal pictured her to have very dark nipples that contrasted beautifully with her milky white skin. She imagined her shaven too, smooth like silk with no sign of shaving rash or wax burn, to be perfect. She also imagined that men would play with both her breasts, not just the left.

For the duration of the journey home Crystal tried desperately to rid her mind of a naked Jenny. The more she tried, the more it seemed as though her own personal flaws were being poked fun at. Her breasts were large and had started to sag and occasionally went the odd day without attending to grooming below. A love of chocolate had seen an increase in a dress size or two not to mention the appearance of the much loathed bingo wings. Crystal had become comfortable, perhaps a little too comfortable in her own body. Maybe a change was needed in this aspect of her life too.

By the time Crystal got home her mood had hit rock bottom. All she wanted was to be wrapped up in her lover's arms and be reassured that no matter how she may feel about herself, he loved her unconditionally. One look into the living room confirmed this was not going to happen as he was flat out on the sofa. Crystal grabbed a cushion and hurled it at him. 'Evening my sleepy prince. I'm off for a soak, so can you rustle up some food? Yes! Lovely' and with that took herself upstairs. A few moments later the front door opened and closed. 'Take away!'

Crystal was already out the bath and drying herself when the door went again. Slipping into her dressing gown she joined her man in the living room for his lovingly prepared meal. On the plate tonight, Chinese set menu for two. Half way through the meal Crystal enquired 'Do you love me?' A short acknowledgment followed from a mouth half full of bamboo shoots and noodles. 'Why?' She enquired again. This time there was an uncomfortable silence that seemed to linger in the air. 'Because we're good together' was the eventual response as he took another mouthful. It wasn't quite the answer Crystal was wanting, but it would do for now.

Once the meal was finished, Crystal stood to clear away the empty cartons and in doing so allowed her dressing gown to fall open revealing to her man nothing underneath. As she left for the kitchen he followed, picking her up and sending the rubbish flying. He placed her on the nearby worktop and buried his head between her legs. Though the angles were a little uncomfortable, it felt so right in the ways that mattered. Changing to a standing, bent over position she allowed him to enter her fully. With each forceful thrust her now freely hanging breasts swayed with the motion. Crystal couldn't help but think that Jenny's smaller perkier boobs would be a lot more comfortable right now. This position wasn't working. Her backs of her legs began to ache and her chest was agony. Crystal slipped away and knelt before her man. Stroking vigorously, it didn't take long to finish him off in her mouth. It was true what he had said, they were good together.

Crystal decided an early night was in order, once she had finished cleaning up the strewn mess in the kitchen. She left her man to find whatever amusement he desired opting herself to catch up on some much needed sleep. It came to her easily, much easier than the previous night. Crystal woke fully refreshed, but surprising alone. There was no sign of her man, either in bed or downstairs when she went to find him. Instead a small note on the hallway sideboard simply read, 'Gone to Gym'. With her body confidence a little poke holed from yesterday, Crystal thought about heading to the gym herself. It had been a while since she last went, but it would be nice to work out in a different way with the man she loved. It was as she approached the gym though, absolute horror and rage coursed through her body. Through one of the large exterior windows, there was her man laughing, joking and being all too touchy feely with Jenny.

A sweat broke out over Crystal's already shaking body. She was sat bolt upright having woken for a second time. 'Bad dream, it was just a bad dream.' Beside her lay her sleeping lover, outside it was pitch black. She herself returned to a sleeping position but draped an arm across her man for reassurance. Crystal closed her eyes and began to think of happy thoughts.

Saturday arrived at the third attempt. Crystal woke and decided that she and her man would spend it together by way of her treat. They would first attempt a little retail therapy; dine somewhere sophisticated to then finally take in a movie at the pictures. If tomorrow normality and the mundane had to return, then today she would make special. Crystal looked and her sleeping man and kicked him out of bed. 'Get dressed baby, we're going out. Oh and smart please!'

Crystal put on a short skirt, blouse and jacket combination, while he opted for jeans, tee shirt and jacket. They looked the epitome of designer chic and it was evident the style was heavily influenced by Crystal's love of high fashion. If last night was an endorsement of them being good together, now they could add looking good together as a reason. As they made their way to the station, Crystal placed her hand in his as if to further endorse her ownership.

Their first stop was to indulge in a spot of window shopping. Whilst she had every intention of coming home with bags full of new, probably unneeded stuff, there was enjoyment to be had wistfully looking amongst that which she couldn't afford. Yesterday's little lunchtime shopping expedition a prime example. Even with a love for high end fashion, Crystal was sensible enough to know that she could obtain several outfits for the price of one if she parted with her money in the right shops.

The two, still hand in hand, made their way through the bustling streets. They would occasionally stop to look around certain shops, some for Crystal and some solely for her man, but with bags now starting to accumulate they decided that perhaps it was time to bring an end to the indulgent spending spree and find somewhere to eat. They settled on a little Italian restaurant just off the main square, with candle lit tables and waiter service. Definitely the sophistication Crystal felt she deserved.

For the first time in long while it felt to Crystal as if the romance had finally returned to their relationship. Though there wasn't the gentlemanly conduct as shown by Sean during their lunch dates, it was a glimmer of the heaven she had been seeking. And although conversation wasn't exactly flowing, there wasn't the usual mealtime silence. 'Do you see us married with kids?' she suddenly enquired, perhaps as a result of the wine being consumed all too easily. There was a choke and a silence as if the right words were being arranged within his head before spoken. It was all she needed to hear, 'I'd like to go home now please.'

The entire journey home was made in silence. The small glimmer of heaven she had seen on the horizon was now the stormy clouds of doubt and confusion. Crystal blamed herself and her over zealousness, as he clearly isn't ready to make such a life commitment. Why would he be? Would he ever be? She thought that it wouldn't now be a surprise if he decided to make a run for it. When they finally got home, Crystal apologised for the wine talking and offered to finish the night cuddled on the sofa. No mention was made again of the incident.

By the time morning arrived, the mundane routines had already started. Her man was busy readying himself for the gym and it was evident the events of yesterday were going to go unspoken. Crystal had the day to herself and her chores, seeing him later that evening. If it wasn't for the guilt and downheartedness she was feeling, it was if it was just another one of her bad dreams. As he left, crystal offered tamely 'I love you' to which 'you too' came his response. It seemed like heaven was clinging on to be reached, even if it was by the fingertips.

Crystal decided the best way forward was to throw herself into her chores. With music on, she scrubbed and cleaned the house from top to bottom. There was no clutter, no mess and everything had a home. She knew it would never last, but for the few hours it would, it was a marvel to behold. She had even unpacked all the shopping they had bought and put it all where they should be, out of sight. With her chores finished and feeling much more like her old self Crystal kicked back and dived into one of the new books she bought this past Friday lunch. If her own slice of personal heaven was proving hard to reach, she could at least read about someone else finding theirs.

Although Crystal was able to lose herself in a good book for hours on end, she was still fully aware of what was expected of her. The tea was cooking and would be ready for when her man returned and she had changed from her scruffs into something a little more appealing on the eye. It was a conscious decision to show him exactly what he had and that he had no need to look elsewhere. If he wasn't ready for commitment now, then Crystal was determined to be the one he said yes too when he was.

He returned on time and they sat in silence eating the food she had lovingly prepared. The fact she was sat eating with him in just her lingerie seemed to go unnoticed, as did the fact she had spent the best part of the day cleaning. Once the meal was over Crystal collected the plates and headed to the kitchen so as to wash up. Half expecting to be followed she waited a little before turning the taps. Instead there were footsteps on the stairs and shortly after a door shutting. It would appear this time she was well and truly in the dog house.

When it came time for Crystal to head for bed, she did so with a certain amount of trepidation as to the response she would get. She opened the door slowly expecting a cold shoulder or for sleep to have already taken her man.

Instead he was lying on the bed full naked and wonderfully erect. 'What took you so long?' he enquired with a broad grin. Crystal ran and jumped on the bed, and then on top of him. She dragged her nails across his smooth ripped chest. 'Well aren't we the mischievous one? How did you know I would come to bed?' There was no answer and he pulled her to him and kissed her passionately.

Crystal could feel him hard between her legs and she could also feel herself getting more and more turned on. Pulling aside her skimpy lace knickers, she squirmed herself into a position that meant the whole of him slid straight within her. Bracing herself and grabbing the bed sheet with both hands she allowed him to control the speed and intensity of their actions. They continued to kiss passionately throughout and even when they both reached their respective climax, the kissing continued long into the night. Eventually sleep took them both as they lay wrapped in each other's arms. For Crystal, there were no bad dreams during this night's sleep.

Monday morning arrived and the 7am alarm woke a blissful and content Crystal. She placed a kiss upon the cheek of her still sleeping lover and started the routine that came with getting ready for work. Today she was feeling sexy and loved and so picked out a risky little number for the office. 'To Hell with the gossip' she declared slipping herself into a plunging v neck top and little black skirt. Half tempted to go with the stockings again a little caution changed her mind to tights instead. Crystal looked herself over in the mirror and couldn't help but smile at how wonderfully cute she thought she looked.

The journey to work did nothing to change Crystal's mood being the usual Monday busy commute. Even work itself was on the surface a mildly interesting day. All of the gossip was focused on the appraisals that were rapidly approaching with some talking of big changes afoot. The phone was a constant distraction from staring at the computer screen all day while the clock hands seemed to turn with unusual haste. Even Jenny with all her bubbliness could not take the smile from Crystal's face. For once she was daring to believe that her little piece of heaven had survived gripping on and was ready to force itself back into her future.

Standing on a packed train at the end of a busy day was not Crystal's idea of fun. The fact she was standing when men were seated proved that the age of chivalry was indeed dead and the likes of Sean were a dying breed. The train ride home was made even more unpleasant by the occasional grope as passengers moved around to either get on or off. Crystal had had enough and as one poor man unfortunately grabbed her breast whilst reaching for an upright, she looked him dead in the eye, 'If only you had asked nicely I would have exposed it for you.' Blushing, the man apologised profusely and made his way further down the carriage. 'Anyone else fancies a cheeky squeeze?' she asked her onlookers. Crystal couldn't help but smile at the small show of hands.

When the train stopped at Crystal's stop, she departed to make the short walk home as she had done many times before. For some reason a nervousness washed over her and put a cold chill down her spine. Even though there were other people milling about on the platform, she couldn't shake the overwhelming feeling of being vulnerable and alone. It felt as if someone was watching her intently and though she scanned around, she could not pin point the person responsible for putting her on edge. Reaching for her phone, she tried in vain contacting her man to come meet her. With no reply it dawned on her she was going to have to make the short trip alone. Trembling and afraid Crystal stayed close to others as best she could whilst jumping at every slight nudge as people past. Fighting back the tears having reached the sanctuary of home she immediately locked and bolted the door behind her.

There was no sign of life, but the unmistakable sound of running water from the bathroom told her there was a beautifully naked man in her shower. Crystal tried to compose herself and wiped away any stray tears before walking in. She hadn't done a very good job because the minute he set eyes on her he asked 'What's up with you?' She explained about the feeling of being watched and the fear that she may be followed home. He simply smiled from the cubicle and replied 'Looking like that babe, I'd have followed you home!' Crystal immediately went from the feeling of being cute and sexy as she had that morning, to that of a cheap hooker. It was not the compassion she was looking for from a man that was supposed to love her. Quickly she changed into something more relaxed and that exposed less, then made her way back downstairs to start the tea.

With the two of them sat with food in front of them, Crystal tried again to explain how uncomfortable she felt at walking home that evening. She continued that it was as if someone was either waiting for her at the station or followed her off the train. Whilst she was probably being irrational and did not actually see anyone, Crystal pleaded with her man to meet her off the train tomorrow. Begrudgingly he agreed although could not hide the fact he felt she was being a little mellow dramatic. For the rest of the evening they cuddled on the sofa. Crystal always felt safe wrapped up in his arms and when the time came for sleep arrived, she continued to wrap herself into him.

Another new day and Crystal woke at the sound of the alarm. Fresh in her mind the way she was made to feel about her choice of clothes yesterday, so decided today would be a simple trouser suit affair. She readied herself for work and kissed her waking man goodbye whilst also reminding him to meet her at the station. His face disappeared back under the duvet as she left for work.

Feeling a little less anxious with it being a glorious sunny day Crystal made the entire journey to work without any re-occurrence of yesterday's emotions. Her mood was further buoyed by thoughts of seeing Sean the next day and being able to pass on the great news from her favourite bookshop. Wondering how long it would take for Sean to come up with more, she hoped it wouldn't be too long before his efforts saw rewards.

The only downside with the weather being good was being greeted by an almost covered perky pair of breasts with nipples that looked like you could use them for coat hooks. Not only were Jenny's breasts bordering on escape, her arse in that skirt was too. If it wasn't for the fact that she envied here so much, there may have been cause for disgust in the way she flaunted herself about. Crystal was pretty sure she wasn't the only one to have imagined her naked, although in that outfit, she practically was.

Work for the most part was a case of same old, same old. Various independent shops had found the going tough and closed, so these properties needed to be found new tenants, whilst there was a mountain of letters and reports that needed typing up and filing. Crystal found herself in quite a privileged position within the company, and was party to many confidential circulations from the upper management. It seemed of late, they were getting very excited about a project that was so hush hush that even she wasn't fully aware of the details. Crystal was pretty sure the impending appraisals would hold a more significant purpose in relation to this project though. Whatever it was, it could only be good for the company based on the little she had read to date.

Adding fuel to the fire, Crystal was asked to make a hotel reservation for two *guests* this coming Thursday, as they would be part of the appraisal panel. This was a new twist on past assessments which were usually a low key one on one affair. She fought back the urge to discuss everything with colleagues as she knew first hand just how the rumour mill in worked. A quiet word here, a whisper there and before you finished the last word the whole office knew. As she sat watching Jenny leaning over and displaying all to a young male apprentice, Crystal thought that maybe something's are best kept secret.

With the time edging towards that of home, the nerves that were more or less absent this morning had started to return. Crystal hoped beyond hope that her man would stay true to his word and meet her off the train. She left work and headed to the station, however upon her arrival all trains had been suspended awaiting further details. Panic began take hold as the thought of having to wait for a later train would mean being late for the meet up with her man and if he gave up waiting, that would mean she would have to walk home alone again. The very thought of such a thing produced tears in her eyes. There was no other option but to take a taxi she thought. It was going to cost her almost four times that of her already paid ticket, but it was worth every penny to arrive safely at her front door. Once one her way she thought she had better text her man the change of plan.

Crystal returned home to find several police cars and an ambulance further up the street. As she left the taxi her man greeted her with the grim news of what was happening as he hugged her in state of obvious relief. Word coming from the scene was that a young woman had been followed off the train and sexually assaulted in an alleyway, though she was in most respects okay, her assailant had fallen victim to his own blade in the struggle. Crystal wept and shook at the realisation that the poor girl could so easily have been her.

It was several hours before Crystal felt she was able to leave the comfort and security of her lover's arms. They sat on the sofa and tried to ignore the world outside their own four walls. She looked him the eye confessed to him her feelings and emotions. 'I love you so much that I couldn't imagine a day when you're not either by my side, or here to come home to. I want us to spend the rest of our lives together and when you're ready we can plan to start a family.' The words had been playing around in her mind whilst they cuddled and she felt in light of recent events the time was right to say them. She couldn't have been more wrong as he stood from the sofa and retorted, 'I love you but I'm never getting married, and don't think for one minute I want to be a dad. If you want to play happy families then baby I'm not your man.' The tears found their way back to Crystal's eyes as he continued, 'You'll have to decide if what we have now is good enough, because for me it's all I want.' She ran to the bedroom and slammed the door behind, tears now flowing like a river that had burst its banks.

Not for the first time Crystal found herself lying awake thinking about her relationship and again not for the first time Sean's whispered words rang loud in her ears. From the sound of the games console downstairs it was obvious the decision was hers and hers alone. What was it she wanted? What were her dreams and goals? Was she ever going to become a fairy princess? In her heart of hearts she knew, and in truth she had known for a while, that sacrifices were going to have to be made.

The morning arrived in usual manner, however unexpectedly Crystal woke alone. Mixed emotions toyed with her mind as the happy side knew she would be seeing Sean for lunch, and yet the sad side reminded her of the dilemma she now found herself in with regards her love life. Crystal showered and readied herself for work in a flowery summer dress and cardigan, knowing eventually she would have to find her man and confront the aftermath of the night before. He was on the sofa asleep with the games machine playing away to itself. Despite everything, Crystal couldn't help but feel the tug of her heartstrings as she gazed upon him. He was a beautiful man trapped with boyish ideals and she loved him.

As Crystal made her way to the station a sombre chill washed over her as she passed the cordoned off area that saw such chilling scenes last night. A news reporter tried to stop her for an interview, but she refused to comment and made haste for her train. She knew he was only doing his job and there was a story to be told, it wasn't hers to tell. When the train arrived, she frantically looked along the carriages to see if Sean was aboard, but sadly she was to be disappointed.

Today was a day that had to have chocolate in it and with that in mind the short detour before work was observed. Feeling particularly down Crystal decided one bar wasn't going to be enough and so a shopping bag was rammed with the contents of a chocoholic's wet dream. Suitably equipped to see out the day, Crystal made the remaining short trip to the office. Today was also a day for putting her head down and trying to suppress the voices rattling around in her mind. It would be a day of targets, and the first was the half ten tea break. Then it would be lunch and meeting Sean, followed by the three o'clock break then home. Crystal emptied her chocolate stash into her drawer, grabbed and report and started typing.

So engrossed in her work, Crystal missed not only the mid morning tea break but was also running late for lunch. With haste she made her way to the door as questions from inquisitive colleagues fell on deaf ears. She continued to run until she stood outside their agreed rendezvous where she allowed herself a moment of composure before walking in. As expected Sean was already there waiting and also as expected rose from his chair as she approached. He offered a courteous kiss to the side of the cheek, although that in itself was not expected, she accepted graciously. It was tender and his lips were incredibly soft. Crystal began to tingle a little inside.

Before they got too engrossed in talk there was a couple of things she wanted to say and in true Crystal style she just came right and said what was on her mind. 'The lunch today is on me being as I am quite certain you paid on the last two occasions, and the piece of writing you wrote, if you were to finish it as a full story then I know where it will sell.' Sean sat trying to digest the two pieces of information as separate points of fact. There seemed very little point in arguing the first, as she was indeed correct and also intent on repaying the deed, the second however was more intriguing and Sean enquired to know more.

Crystal retold of how she had come to ask about having Sean's work sold in the little bookshop, that the bookstore owner had passed favourable comment on the part he had read. 'All you have to do is finish it!' she remarked enthusiastically. Sean looked at her in a way a parent may gaze upon a child attempting something for the first time. 'Every good story must have a sound beginning to draw you in, a middle to sustain interest and a finish that is memorable. As this opening little paragraph is about us, I wonder then what of our middle and indeed our end?' he asked whimsically. Crystal stared at him intently in almost silence before offering a reply she wished she had thought about first, 'you write it and we will act it out.' Sean raised an eyebrow and laughed.

Sean handed Crystal another piece of paper explaining that he also loved to try his hand at poetic verse, that it gave him the chance to tell a story in much fewer words. With an excited smile she back and read.

He swoops down upon wings blacker than the darkest of nights With the precision of an arrow from a marksman's bow Thirst driving him onward to take his chosen prey All they will know is the quick sharp pain of his final blow

Now he feasts upon the life force of his human victim The thick red liquid still warm and sweet as he gulps it down There will be no savouring this first meal since his awakening But he'll make sure not even a drop splashes down on the ground

A light in the distance coming closer disturbs his feeding With haste he takes flight taking refuge within the darkness of night Looking down he observes the consequences of his actions With a blood stained smile he turns away and takes flight

Crystal looked visibly disturbed even through a forced smile after finishing the piece, images of the night before going through her head with each line read. Though she knew it was complete fiction and vampires didn't roam the night's sky, it was on the same hand a little too close in timing. Sean too seemed disturbed at having upset her in some way with what he had written. Crystal thought it best to explain the events that were still leaving her emotionally scared.

As the time ticked ever closer to the end of lunch so Crystal's nerves calmed. Though it hadn't been the intense meetings of minds they shared during previous lunches, she had seen another facet to Sean's personality. He possessed a caring nurturing side and was able to show compassion when he felt it was needed. He was indeed a true gentleman and there was no doubt in her mind, that despite his years he would make a wonderful father. Crystal pictured him telling stories he himself had written to the children before bed, helping them with their homework as they grew older, all the while being a dutiful husband to a wife that loved him. Sean's gesturing brought her from her thoughts. 'Shall we meet again here? Or would you like a change of scenery? I know a lovely little Italian restaurant not far.' Crystal's mind went blank and simply agreed to meet again here. Sean placed a kiss upon her cheek as he had done earlier and they left to go their separate ways.

All afternoon Crystal couldn't shake the meeting with Sean from her mind. 'First he writes a poem harrowing similar to the horrible events of last night. Was it mere coincidence? Then he asks if we would like to change to the same Italian restaurant we were at on Saturday. Could it be coincidence again?' Her head was in a spin. With a rational mind it all seemed very plausible that what just transpired was a series of coincidental events totally unrelated to previous events. In Crystal's current mindset he was nothing more than some kind of stalker and there was no way they were meeting again.

Crystal's world, in the space of a few weeks, had turned to absolute turmoil. At home was a man she desperately loved, always wanted to fuck and yet their paths seemed destined to head in search of different dreams. Wednesdays were for a man who could give her everything mentally and she enjoyed being with, and yet dark clouds loom over with the possibility he could be a little infatuated. 'So much for his writing being his only mistress' she thought. All she needed now was for her appraisal to go horribly wrong on Friday and find herself in the dole queue. Crystal took another bar of chocolate from her drawer and sighed heavily. Heaven it seemed was a grain of sand in a vast sprawling desert waiting to be found.

The time for home came and went. As much as she had put her head down during the morning, Crystal was making a double effort to block out the world since returning from lunch. There were simply too many questions to match up with the answers that swam around in her head. Eventually it was the cleaners wanting to lock up for the night that forced her to abandon her little makeshift sanctuary and head home. As she stood on the near deserted station platform, tears began to roll down her face like raindrops on a window.

As the train pulled to a stop Crystal's platform, she noticed a familiar figure sat waiting for her in the cold night air. True to his word her man had waited almost two hours and saw several trains come and go whilst upholding his promise. With everything that had gone on during the day, she had neglected to tell him of her plan to work late. By now the tears fell more of a torrent as she ran to throw herself into his arms.

The two walked home under a moonlit sky deciding to find somewhere to eat rather than attempt cooking so late. There was a slight nip in the air and she clung close to the side of her man, his arm wrapped tightly round her. They stopped at a small Indian restaurant opting to sit in and eat rather than take it with them. While there was a romantic feel about being met from the train and being taken to out to eat, Crystal missed Sean's gentlemanly conduct as she was left to follow her man to their table and find her own seat. The fact that she was going to end up paying for this meal also hadn't escaped her as he took the liberty of ordering a mountain of food and drink for the both of them.

Crystal sat and watched as the man opposite stuffed himself full of all that was before him. Several empty bottles of larger accompanied the plates being stacked at one side as they too were being stripped of their contents. She couldn't stop her mind from wandering to how, no more than eight hours ago, she was sat facing food with another and yet conversation flowed more than the alcohol. Had she judged him too hastily? All she knew right now was that she was missing his company.

Suitably fed and watered Crystal settled the bill before leaving to return home. It had become quite late in the evening and all she could think about was getting under the duvet in the hope that sleep would find her. She also prayed that her man, now full of curry and larger, was of the same mind as the last thing she wanted was a drunken fuck to confuse her further. Luckily he never made it further than the living room, instead passing out on the sofa. Crystal rolled her eyes and retired to the comfort of her bed.

Crystal starred through bleary eyes at clock which told her it was nearer the time she came to bed, than that of getting up. At the end of the bed her still drunken lover was fighting a losing battle with his clothes in an attempt to come to bed. Crystal got up and helped strip him off. 'I love you' he offered falling into bed. 'As I you baby' she replied lying back down beside him. Before she had time to adjust the bed sheets he had fallen asleep and was snoring loudly. Placing her head upon his chest and wrapping an arm around him, Crystal too found sleep came quickly.

As a new day dawned Crystal woke to the sensation of her inside leg being gently nibbled. Her man teased the parts he knew would make her squirm, concentrating on the inner thigh and lower stomach. Crystal fought to free herself from his tormenting all the while laughing loudly with his every touch. The two played, rolling around the bed until the realisation of the time meant getting ready for work became the main focus. As she stood to walk to the bathroom, a pillow followed and connected with the back of her head.

Suitably dressed and fed, she kissed her man goodbye and started on the familiar journey into work. It was another fine sunny day which only helped keep her in the good spirits her morning frolic had put her in. As the train pulled to a stop, Crystal was caught in full surprise to see Sean stood smiling at her. 'Are you some kind of stalker?' She blurted out boarding the carriage. Sean could not help but laugh explaining that he had been invited to a magazine where they were interested in publishing some of his short fiction. Blushing greatly, Crystal demanded to know more as they continued their journey together.

It was Sean who left the train first leaving Crystal to take next three stops alone. As they parted ways she wished him luck and could not wait to hear how it went when they next met. It was amazing how being back in his company, even for the briefest of times made her feel so much more stimulated inside. If there were any lingering doubts about Sean being an infatuated stalker, then they had been well and truly buried within her sub conscience. All she could think about now was them meeting up next week and being able to read his work in print.

Arriving at the office the mood was subdued and almost morgue like. There was no idle gossip around the tea machine and no staff just milling around trying to avoid work. It was certainly a good indication that people were on tender hooks over tomorrow's appraisals. As Crystal sat at her desk ready for another nose to the grind stone, block out the world day, the whispers reached her of two strangers having arrived early that morning. She could only surmise that they were the ones she had booked a hotel for earlier in the week.

It was not long before they were walking around on a meet and greet being introduced to all the staff. The first, Mr Lavkin was quite insignificant by appearance. Medium height and build with short cropped dark hair, he was dressed in a bland dark suit that could quite easily have been bought from any high street store. The second was, by contrast, a veritable dream. Mr Munoz stood tall with long oiled black hair, olive skin and a body that was definitely on par with that of her man's. Dressed in a pair of jeans and white shirt, he cut a very fine figure for a man indeed and Crystal was very aware of the fact she was staring, but she could not take her gaze away. 'Now there is a man that wouldn't neglect the right nipple' she thought.

It was Mr Lavkin that introduced himself first as professionalism returned once more to a lust filled Crystal.

As far as she could tell he was a Director for the company, which in itself was quite odd as this was the first time she had seen or met him. Mr Munoz was also in retail development and this could only suggest a take-over of some sort was being planned. None of this mattered to Crystal of course, just that she could to hear him speak whilst having the privilege of touching him, albeit by handshake. She lost herself in his eyes as, for that moment at least, her man and Sean faded into insignificant people in her life.

By the time lunch arrived the mood in the office had lifted and gossip was rife. It seemed Crystal was not the only one taken with their Spanish guest, with talk amongst the females being along the lines of what they would and wouldn't do to such a man. It was clearly evident that the 'would' far outnumbered the 'would not' and she could not help but agree. The males however were probably right in their concern over what the visit meant in terms of the office and indeed their careers.

All afternoon the two men sat in various meeting with senior members of the company, occasionally conducting private meetings between themselves. It would have been hard to say just how much actual work was carried out across all the staff, as all eyes seemed to be on proceedings and from a female perspective one certain Spanish arse. Such were the length of the meetings that they were still being conducted as time for home arrived. There was no use in speculating what was happening and it seemed the general consensus that all would become clear tomorrow, fingers crossed.

As Crystal stood waiting for her train, the two men actively present in her life came back to mind. If Sean was indeed a stalker as she thought yesterday, then he would be on this train. As it arrived she looked up and down the carriages but to mixed emotions there was no sign. She also wondered if at the end, her man would be waiting as he had previously, regardless he was in for a treat when she got home. Whether it was the Spanish influence or not she wasn't sure but she was feeling in the mood for pure unadulterated sex.

He was indeed waiting on the platform for her to return and once she was able, Crystal grabbed him by the hand and at double speed led him home. The door was no sooner shut before she started stripping him down along with herself. Completely naked she manoeuvred him to the stairs and pushed him back, taking his erection in her hand and stroking it gently. Crystal continued to tease with the tongue over the tip before taking it fully in her mouth. There were groans coming from them both as she continued to bring him to the point of climax, but then stopping short. She changed positions and pulled at his head as he now repaid her for that which she had done to him. Crystal groaned loudly as he missed his timing. With legs shaking, she motioned they move up to the bedroom. Obligingly he helped her up the remaining stairs and threw her on the bed. The foreplay was definitely over as he joined her on the bed and got on top. Sinking himself fully into her, Crystal let out a louder groan and begged for it to be hard and fast, which he duly did. The sheer bliss made her head spin with every thrust until this time his timings were spot on. A simultaneous climax saw them collapse in heap, breathing heavily but both totally satisfied.

They both decided to share a shower, each soaping the other and tenderly wiping them down. If the sex was pure primal urge, then this was a little hint of romance. Suitably clean and covered the two of them retired back downstairs for a bite to eat. Rustling up something both quick and not too filling, Crystal felt that all in all the day had been a very one indeed. As routine dictated, they sat in silence and ate.

Before retiring to sleep and leaving her man to his sport, Crystal rummaged around her wardrobes for the perfect outfit for tomorrow. It had to show a dedicate professional and yet if *he was* going to be there, then why not a little of her flirty side. She could not believe herself and a sudden wave of guilt descended on her. Having just had some of the best sex in days, here she was thinking of flirting with another man she had just met. Her thoughts flashed back to the skirt and stockings she wore on only the second date with Sean and the day trouble they caused. 'I am such a bad woman at times' she laughed settling on a trouser suit and low cut top ensemble.

7am arrived and the sound of the alarm was muted seconds after starting. Crystal lay awake on the bed watching the sun breaking through the small gap in the curtains. It was Friday and that meant her appraisal along with, if what she had been told was right, news of the promotion she had been put forward for. Butterflies fluttered around her stomach with nerves at just exactly what she was going to be told. Cuddling into her man for a reassuring hug, Crystal was putting off getting ready until the very last minute.

Crystal dressed to impress and then turned her attention to her man. Kissing him tenderly till he woke, she said her goodbyes and asked 'Going to wish me luck?' The confused look on his face brought the realisation to her that they had not discussed anything of what was happening today. In fact they hadn't really talked about much of what was going on in each other's lives the past few weeks. She smiled and upon leaving the bedroom whispered 'Forget it baby. Love you.' His response trailed off to a mumble as descended the stairs. Too nervous to eat, she left the house and made her was in the glorious sunshine to the station.

The train ride was a quiet affair with Crystal allowed to seat herself and ponder yet further. So deep in thought was she that it escaped her notice the view others were getting down her top, especially those that chose to stand in close proximity. It was arriving at her stop that some clarity returned to the situation. She turned to one particular man whose mouth was hanging open as he stared at her cleavage, 'You can have the right nipple if you want, my boyfriend isn't so keen on that one.' Crystal winked in his direction as she left the train, and watched as he averted his gaze and wiped at his mouth.

'One thousand, seven hundred and forty three' Crystal muttered as she stood at the door to the office. She took in a deep breath and walked through. As she expected there were a couple of comments aimed at her regarding being first in the firing line, but she ignored them as always and sat herself at her desk. She kept telling herself over and over that she was going to be fine and to remember she was commended not too long ago. It still did nothing to settle the still fluttering butterflies.

'Crystal. Would you please join us?' came the dreaded line from her manager's office. Nervously she stood and exhaled a huge breath of air before walking over. Surprisingly she was offered words of support and good luck from her colleagues as she passed them to join those she would be appraised by. In the office already were a seated Mr Lavkin and Munoz and joining them her own boss Mr Hines. Crystal took to a seat opposite and braced herself.

The appraisal part went incredibly well. Her boss could not sing her praises any better had he been in the church choir. The entire time she was in the office, Crystal tried desperately not to stare directly across at Mr Munoz, even though it was blatantly obvious his gaze was at times firmly fixed upon her chest. She found it also hard to fight the impure thoughts of what she would do had it just been the two of them in the office. In the first instance her boss's table looked incredibly sturdy.

Conversation turned to that of the intended promotion, and that was where *he* and Mr Lavkin came in. Plans were being drawn up to open a second office in southern Spain so as to take benefit of the increasing demand for real estate for the hospitality industry. 'We would very much like for you to join us in this new office Crystal and work alongside Mr Lavkin and Munoz while they build up the company portfolio in Spain.' explained her boss. 'It would be an honour to work with you Crystal' remarked Mr Munoz. There was a stunned silence coming from the chair in which she sat.

Mr Lavkin interjected the awkward pause in proceedings and stated he understood what a monumental decision it was that they were placing upon her, but they would very much like to get things underway sooner rather than later. 'Crystal. Go back to work now and think it over during the weekend. We will talk again on Monday and you can let me know what you think.' stated her boss. 'I'm sure you have a lot to think about, but whatever you decide, we will respect your opinion. Thank you Crystal.'

Still in a state of shock she returned to her desk as the next person was called for. Her colleagues quizzed her for information about what to expect, but she could say nothing. There were a multitude of colliding thoughts racing around inside her head. Spain! She had not seen that coming, even with the arrival of Mr Munoz. What of her man? Would he follow her? What of Sean? Would she have time to meet him one last time before she went? Was she evening wanting to go?

Crystal took a bar of chocolate left from the other day out of her drawer and took a bite. 'Well I prayed for a break from the monotony that was my life' she said. 'Don't be afraid to chase my dreams Sean said.' She took another bite. 'He doesn't want to marry me or have children' she thought out loud. 'I wonder if I can get through customs in a fairy princess outfit' she laughed to herself.

The journey home saw Crystal deep in contemplation over the amazing opportunity she had been offered. It would certainly be a chance to break from the mundane cycle she had wished to free herself, but recently since meeting Sean, there was now that escape. Crystal hoped that she would have a chance to see Sean should she decide to go, and of course she would have to find a way to break it her man. If their recent attempts at communication were any indication, this may just be the hardest part.

As the train entered Crystal's platform, there for a second night running her man was stood waiting for her. It was moments like this that made her feel certain that despite his faults, deep down there was a good guy inside and it was these moments that made her love him all the more. As she approached, she flung her arms around his neck and she kissed him passionately. 'I have some news to tell you and so we are going to have to sit down and talk about it.' she gestured before attempting to go back to their kissing. A look of horror was instantly visible across his face, 'You're not pregnant are you?' Crystal took him by the hand. 'We'll talk about it when we get home.'

If the plan was to sow a seed and watch it grow, then it worked. No sooner were they home and the door shut behind them, the inquiry began. 'At least let me change and start the tea' Crystal chuckled. Her man's face was now awash with frustration pleading that she at least part with a hint as to what was so important. She had to admit that if it had been this easy getting a conversation going, she would have adopted the method ages ago. There was also a certain enjoyment to be had keeping him guessing too.

They both convened in the kitchen so that Crystal could prepare the evening meal and as promised, fill her man in on the events of her day and the news she wished to discuss. 'What do you think to Spain?' she teasingly began. 'We're going on holiday? That's what you wanted to talk about?' he replied with a somewhat uninterested tone. 'Well, more to live'' she returned not lifting her gaze from preparing the food. With her man suitably confused, Crystal began to elaborate on the offer she had been presented and that if she were to accept, then it was her wish they went together. There was no mistaking the enthusiasm in her man his time. 'Oh the lads are going to be so jealous when I tell them on Sunday'

Though it wasn't the discussion she had hoped, it was at least the confirmation she wanted that if she were to go, the journey would not be made alone. All that remained now was to either meet Sean next week and tell him of her offer, or at least somehow get word to him. The last thing she wanted was to just vanish with no explanation, of course assuming she accepted the offer. There was always the option to just stay with the devil she knew and carry on with her current life. It was going to prove to be a weekend of much answer finding.

When eventually it was time for sleep, Crystal cuddled up into the back of her man and asked 'So do you think I should take the promotion?' He rolled over to face her and replied in surprise 'How could you not take it? Turn down the chance to live and work with a place in the sun, not to mention the siestas. Oh no, I think we should definitely go.' Crystal smiled and kissed him gently on the cheek. 'Then I guess we're going to need to sort a lot of things out. Like what to do with this place, what to take with us, what to…' It was no use continuing as already her words were falling on deaf ears as her man slept. Crystal rolled over and stared at the ceiling. Sleep was going to elude her again as preparations were being planned in her already crammed full mind. It was certain, she would take the offer and they were off to Spain.

Saturday was to be a day for check lists and planning. It was obvious from the lack of help that this was going to be a very one sided affair and one that would involve turning the house into complete chaos. Crystal had decided that in order to maintain some kind of backup should all go wrong, the house would be put up for rent through her company, one of the perks of working in real estate. It would give them a roof should they return, whilst also meaning they could forget about it whilst away. 'It's probably good that one of us in this relationship has their head on' she mumbled as she moved onto the next item on the list. Passports sorted, suitcases found and clothes sorted through, the day was turning out to be a very productive one. It was probably helped that her man was out of the way watching football on the TV.

As the day turned into evening, several boxes had been filled with belongings that needed a new home, whilst those to be taken sat in the bedroom beside the cases. Crystal stood impressed viewing the fruits of her labour, and even more impressed that her man had thoughtfully rustled up the evening tea. It was by no means nouvelle cuisine, but hot edible and not something else she'd had to do. 'Perhaps this will be the start of seeing the man in her man' she thought. That night she slept soundly the questions that previously plagued her mind finally silenced.

If yesterday was all about planning for a new beginning, then today was a case of same old same old. Crystal woke late to find her man had already left for the gym. It would now be several hours before she would see him again, and perfect for her to continue from where she left things. She would also have to find time to prepare the full Sunday roast, 'It may be awhile till we get to eat one of those again' she mused. By the time her man returned home that evening, everything was practically sorted. Ignoring the furniture and fixtures, there wasn't a great deal left. Neither of them was known for keeping sentimental keepsakes and both enjoyed a minimalistic approach to décor. Her approach was that of anything they may need but did not have room for, they would buy again out there.

Crystal had prepared a full roast dinner with all the trimmings with the only thing missing a table to set. Food has always been consumed on their laps in front of the TV, something she hoped she could change in their new home. She hoped to change the silence between them too although she had continually tried to no avail. 'Perhaps it's true that men cannot multi task' she thought. At least the devouring of everything on his plates was confirmation he appreciated her cooking. Clearing away the plates Crystal could not help but wonder if he was in the mood of devouring her if she served herself up as desert.

The evening for Crystal was seen out snug and warm in bed lost in the words of a good book. With all the chores down and all the leaving preparations done, she felt she owed it to herself to have a little relaxation time whilst her man was still downstairs engrossed in the TV. It had always amazed her how he could play the sport, watch and talk about the sport and yet still come home and re-watch the sport. She went without desert this evening however as sleep found her before her man did.

Crystal woke and stared at the grey bleak sky outside. It had also started to rain. She had hoped for better weather given that she was heading into work to give the green light to the start of a new life. 'This better not be an omen' she muttered wearily. Her man had also woken and whilst trying to tempt her back into bed, was offering to put the smile on her on face that the weather hadn't. She looked at him as he lay there and could not help but think 'I'm really not in the mood.' Perhaps there comes a time in a relationship when a little added spice is needed. The sex for the most part was good, more than good, but it was becoming a little too predictable. It was very much a case of the left breast syndrome. Instead Crystal resorted to smiling and replying 'It's *that* time baby' and made her way to the bathroom.

After having dressed suitably for the weather and finding that rare amount of time to fit in some breakfast, Crystal shouted up her goodbyes and set off on her journey to work. Though she wondered how many more times she would make this particular trip and how, in a way, she would miss it, what she would not miss was the inclement English weather. In her mind, no matter who you were, it was impossible to feel good and look sexy knowing you are about to be crammed on a busy train with a host of other drowned rats.

No sooner had Crystal arrived at work and sat herself at her desk with a cup of tea, her boss appeared at his door and summoned her to his office. This was guaranteed to have the tongues wagging, especially after the appraisals last Friday. 'Take a seat Crystal' gestured Mr Hines. 'I understand the speed at which we have asked you to make such an important decision, however time in business never stands idle. At first we would like you to go over for a month in order to find your feet, you can take a partner of friend to help you acclimatise if you so wish. Mr Munoz has kindly offered you a place to stay in his family home whilst a more permanent home can be found. Then, once you return in a month we can appraise the role further.' There was a short pause while she tried to take in everything her boss had just said. 'Well?' he enquired 'Will we be seeing you here next week?' Crystal shook her head, 'No! I'd be honoured to take the role.'

The time had started to encroach into lunch by the time Crystal left her boss' office, such was the magnitude of finer details they had to sort and finalise. She had learned well in all her time working for Mr Hines to cross the Ts and dot the Is as far as negotiations were concerned. Aware that she would be expected to spill the beans to her nosey co-workers, instead of returning to her desk, she decided to have her lunch out.

Crystal returned to work somewhat bedraggled, the weather abating further since her morning commute. As expected the gossip train was powering along at full speed, herself being the focal point once more. That was, until Jenny was summoned in Mr Hines' office. It was the first time Crystal had ever recalled seeing the fire extinguished in her personality. Gone was her bubbly hyper child like demeanour, instead she cut a rather deflated and dejected figure as she made her way across the office. Where there had only ever been envy as a felt emotion, Crystal could not help but now feel a little sorry for her. Innocence of youth can only be your defence for so long, eventually there comes a time when you have to accept responsibility for your own actions, as Jenny was about to find out.

The whole office dynamic changed after Jenny had collected her things and left. It was as if the very heart beat of the place was packed away in her box of belongings and disappeared out the door with her. Crystal could not help but feel disgusted that of the two protagonists, the Indian was made to walk whilst the Chief remained in power, but then when you play with fire one is bound to get burnt. One thing she was not going to miss were those perky pointy nipples that greeted you on a regular basis.

When the time for home came, the return journey was a much more pleasurable one to that taken this morning. The trains were running on time, the rain had stopped and it was approaching another day closer to starting her new life in sunny Spain. Crystal lost herself in thoughts of sunning herself by the side of a pool during afternoon siesta whilst sipping sangria and eating tapas. 'Oh yes, I could so get used to a life like that' she said to herself, however the arrival at her stop on the train brought her back to reality with a bump. Looking outside it appeared that two days in a row of being escorted home was going to be her lot. A crazy thought flashed before her that he would be home having cooked a wonderful meal for the two of them and would then whisk her upstairs for the desert she missed yesterday. 'At least Spain is real' she sighed walking home alone.

As she approached her door there was a real reluctance to put her key in the lock, such was her anguish at hearing several male voices laughing and joking on the other side. If her thought of returning home to find tea waiting seemed foolish before, now it teetered on the edge of lunacy. As she entered there was an instant drop in volume as a forced hush fell across the lads. Crystal smiled whilst peering into the living room, 'I'll be upstairs if you need me. You boys obviously need a little more time to say your goodbyes.' She offered with a hint of sarcasm. She retired upstairs to find comfort in a hot bath and her book.

The water was cold on Crystal's feet as she sat by the edge of the pool. He had just finished swimming lengths and was lifting himself out of the water, the sun glistening off the droplets across his well muscled olive skinned body. He stood like a bronzed statue in tight small black swim trunks matching the colour of his long dripping wet hair. As she began to imagine the only part of him she could not see neatly packaged in those tiny trunks, as splash of water hit full in the face. Her man had followed her dreamy gaze and was now sending handfuls of water in her direction. Startled Crystal opened her eyes to see her man by the side of the bath splashing water over her. 'Hey there sleepyhead, we've ordered food in if you want to come grab some.' Wiping her face with a cloth, she thought 'These dreams are going to have to stop before they get me into trouble!'

A few slices of pizza, a good book and tucked up in bed alone, not exactly the night Crystal had planned. She thought that perhaps during her lunch break tomorrow a visit to her favourite little bookshop may be required. Firstly, not only would she need something to read on the plane, but also it may be a good idea to polish up on a little Spanish if she was going to be living there. The current extent of her knowledge ran to ordering a couple of drinks and asking to see the menu.

Crystal woke to the sound of someone being rather ill in the bathroom with the very sound churning her stomach. 'You had better clean that up once you're done' she shouted knowing all too well she was going to have to venture in at some point. The door to the bedroom crashed open and a rather sickly looking boyfriend threw himself on the bed groaning like some dying animal. Though it wasn't quite her normal time to get up, the prospect of sharing a bed with *that* did not excite her, nor did the aroma in the bathroom for that matter. Desperately clinging on to her own stomach, she opened a window before jumping in the shower. Suitably dressed and refreshed, Crystal made her way downstairs to find several more bodies strewn across the living room. She was certainly not in the mood to deal with the carnage of the boys all night bender, so left for work without so much as a goodbye, although not before making sure the door closed with a satisfying slam behind her.

The day continued to start badly with the news that all trains had been suspended and replaced with an alternative bus service. This left Crystal with a dilemma. To either take the bus and save a little money but be late for work, or pay the extra for a taxi to get her in on time. She decided that perhaps the latter was the safer option, especially in light of her new promotion and wishing to leave with an unblemished record. If she was lucky, she may even beat the boss in for once.

Crystal arrived at work and made a beeline for the coffee machine. Having left the house almost as soon as she got up, caffeine was most certainly needed if she was going to get through the day. A dull ache in her stomach deflated any raised spirits as she may now be coming down with whatever struck low her man. The thought of the pizza she indulged herself on brought a lump to her throat. Gingerly she made her way to her desk to find an internal Email waiting for her. 'Flights booked for this Saturday at Heathrow, 11am. Mr Munoz will meet you at the other end.' it read.

The entire morning Crystal's thoughts were solely focused on reducing the work piled in her To Do tray. In doing so she became increasingly aware that for the first time ever, it was actually going down. There was no new work arriving to replace that which she had just cleared. 'I better slow down as this won't last me till Friday' she thought, 'but there again, who cares!' This fact had not gone unnoticed by her colleagues either as the gossip began to build momentum as to why. By the time lunch arrived, they ranged from simply 'working her notice' to the more vindictive 'quite clearly the new Jenny'. Crystal ignored them all and as she had promised herself, left the office to pay a visit to her favourite little bookshop.

Just the smell inside the shop put Crystal into a dreamy haze. Had it been an option to spend the rest of the afternoon scouring through the hidden literary gems that filled the shop, she would not have needed to have been asked twice. Her search started in her favourite section, romance. Crystal was a sucker for a good love story and enjoyed nothing more than reading about others finding that little piece of happy ever after. It somehow filled her with hope that one day she too would find it waiting. After looking through a plethora of boxes and bookcases she settled on a novel set against the dark and grim backdrop of Victorian London, the choice heavily inspired by Sean. Before leaving a quick look in the much smaller travel section uncovered a Spanish translation book that would prove to be ideal. Crystal paid for her choices and made the short walk back to work almost dreading the reception she was going to get on her return.

Her fears were unjustified as the rest of her working day passed without so much as a whispered word associated with her name. There was even an increase to her workload that could have silenced the gossip. With just three days left before she departed for her first taste of Spanish living, Crystal wondered as to when she would let her colleagues know. With tomorrow set aside for maintaining contact with Sean, it was probably best to announce things on the Thursday, leaving enough time to say goodbye but not too soon as to have to endure the inquest that was sure to follow. 'Perhaps I'll treat them all to cake as a way to keep them quiet' she thought.

Come home time there was more evidence that the day was going to end better than it had started. The trains were back in service although busy, which meant there was a possible chance her man would be there to meet her, although given he wasn't yesterday her hopes were slim. She also hoped the impromptu sleep over had finished and her home was no longer smelling of sickness and men. The train ride home proved to be an ideal opportunity to start with her learning even though she was very aware of the strange looks she was getting from her every attempt at speaking her chosen phrases. No matter how she tried to pronounce them, it still sounded like an English woman speaking Spanish.

It was another walk home alone, which in truth came as no surprise. It came as no surprise either to find that although the house was tidier than the carnage she left it in this morning, it was only what she would call 'man tidy'. Changing from her work attire to something more comfortable, Crystal set about the chores as any woman would. Once their tea had cooked, she called to her still sleeping man to rejoin the land of the living.

As they sat down to eat Crystal enquired as to how he was now feeling, given that she too had a touch of belly ache earlier in the day. By way of cheering him up, she told him of the good news regarding flying out this coming Saturday. 'What!! Why so soon? Baby I have an important match on Sunday and can't possibly leave before that.' Crystal was dumbfounded and retorted 'Why do you think I have packed everything to go?' Without even faltering in his eating he replied quit curtly 'because you're an organisation freak. I assumed it would be at least a month or so away.' Slamming down her plate in a mix of fury and disappointment Crystal stood and headed for the door with tears forming in her eyes, 'Then I'll go on my own.'

Crystal sobbed heavily on the bed wishing he would come upstairs and make everything better, but she knew he wouldn't. In all the time they had been together, he had never done well with confrontation and her crying. It was going to be up to her to go down and try to sort it out. There comes a time in a relationship when you are forced to step back and re-evaluate the love and commitment given to that being returned. Crystal reluctantly found herself at that time. Already he had knocked back the notion of marriage and children, a deal breaker for most couples, now he was putting a game of football before their long term plans. She loved him very much and never doubted the fact. She doubted though if love alone was enough to keep them together. As she made her way down stairs, she already had the words ready that she knew she needed to say.

Crystal sat herself down on the sofa next to him and waited for the lump in her throat to settle. She looked straight at him and started to pour her heart out. 'You know I love you, with all my heart I sincerely do, but there comes a time when we have to be realistic about what we both want from life.' With no offered response she continued, 'I want to be loved as much as I love, and I do not doubt you love me, but marriage and kids have to be as important to you as they are for me.' This time he stood looked down on her in an almost overpowering stance, 'We've been through all this and you know how I feel, so what has this to do with you storming off in tears?' As he spoke she could feel them returning to her eyes with what she was about to say, 'We want different things. If you won't come with me on Saturday and the football is more important than our future, then as much as it breaks my heart, I think it will be the end of us.' As he continued to stand over he simply replied, 'I won't be leaving on Saturday.' Crystal's tears were now uncontrollable as she got up and fled to the bedroom.

The sound of the morning alarm woke Crystal with a start. She had cried herself to sleep and was still dressed as she was the evening before. It was clear that she spent the night alone as there was no sign of her man having attempted to find her, presumably instead opting to stay downstairs and sleep on the sofa. There was a bittersweet emotion resting uneasily upon Crystal knowing that in one hand her relationship could now be over after their exchange last night, in the other the fact that she would be seeing Sean for the last time before departing for Spain. Today would certainly start to see the foundations for her new life laid and just who cared for her enough to be part of it.

Having dressed ready for work, Crystal made her way downstairs to confront the fallout from the night before. As expected her man lay asleep on the sofa, and for the first time there was now a feeling of acceptance that despite the emotional hold he had over her, she wanted so much more. Nudging him gently so as to rouse him from his slumber, she looked at him and asked 'Have you had a change of heart yet?' He rolled over putting his back towards her replying 'Nope.' Crystal left for work without saying another word.

Any attempts to hide her unhappiness had been unsuccessful evident by the number of people that stopped to ask if she was okay during her journey. 'If it's obvious to strangers, then work will be a nightmare' she thought. Sure enough, no sooner had she walked through the office door the tongues started wagging. In an attempt to defuse the situation before it got out of hand, she announced to everyone her news, 'Friday will be my last day in the office. I've been offered a position abroad and have decided to take it. The tears though are because my boyfriend will not be joining me and so we split up last night. I'm not looking for your sympathy, just to be able to work my last few days in relative peace. Thank you.' Crystal sat at her desk and wiped away any lingering tears. 'Roll on lunch time' she thought. Her announcement had not stopped tongues wagging, but instead of them doing so behind her back, she was confronted with overwhelming support and well wishes. 'I'll get us all some cakes later' she announced 'my farewell treat to you all.' This was met with unanimous approval.

Lunch arrived and Crystal made her usual escape from the office heading straight to her now regular meeting with Sean. She was greeted in usual fashion with him still showing his impeccable gentlemanly conduct. He had already taken the liberty to order food and drink, so their time together could be best spent catching up on what was new since last they met. 'I'm surprised you haven't asked me yet' he said with a hint of disappointment in his tone. Crystal could not help but look at him blankly until he went on to explain about his meeting with the magazine. She had totally forgotten with all that had been going on in her own life of late, and could not apologise enough for forgetting. Sean handed her a copy of the piece that was going to be in print next week, and Crystal could not help but start to read.

My name is Isabelle and this is my diary and written confession. I own a house offering refuge for women who have lost their way in the world and they repay my hospitality by providing paid service to those men that seek intimacy in the arms of a woman. Whilst I see our home as providing a service to those that frequent us regularly, the law would see it otherwise and is why I write this from the confinement of my cell.

Sean explained that every week for four weeks, there would be a different tale coming from the House of Isabelle, a manuscript that was short in its construction and would appeal to most people. As the publishers had told him 'sex sells'. Crystal stopped reading, knowing if she were to continue, the time would get away from them and her own news would go left untold. She put the work to one side and sat so as to look intently at him. 'I have some news of my own.' She started. 'I've been offered the chance to Spain for work and will mean being away initially for four weeks, indefinitely if it all works out.' Sean in his usual calm and collect manner asked if she had decided to take the wonderful opportunity and if so, when did she leave. Her response left him shell shocked. 'Yes. I fly out this Saturday' she confirmed. 'I would love to have your address though so that we can write and stay in touch.' An uncomfortable silence settled between them for a short time, until eventually Sean produced a small piece of paper from his little leather note book and started to write. Once he had finished, he folded the paper and handed it to her lingering his hand upon her touch as she reached to take it from him.

The news clearly unsettled Sean as the normal conversational flow seemed to dry. They both ate in relative silence and Crystal could not help but think the friendship they shared was about to be tested for the second time. The time eventually arrived for Crystal to offer her farewell. She stood and took Sean in her arms. 'I'll write the minute I get there, and you have to promise me you'll write back and let me know how the writing is going.' He agreed and apologised for being so silent. 'Just as our friendship had started to blossom, after fate threw us together, now fate decides to rip us apart. I'll miss you Crystal, but I'm pleased you are chasing your dreams.' The tears started to flow again as they made their way to the door and started to head their separate ways. Crystal turned and called after him, 'Sean! I'll miss you too.'

Returning to the office with an assortment of cream and jam cakes as promised she put them out for everyone near the drinks machine before sitting back at her desk. Not for the first time, Sean's words floated around in her head. Was she really chasing her dreams? Or was the chance to move away just a necessary step in breaking free from the routines that were holding her back from chasing them? Crystal took what she thought was Sean's address from her bag where she had put it.

Every Wednesday at twelve o'clock I shall be here. I will wait upon your return for as long as it takes so that we can talk more as we always have. Never will I forget your face and your beautiful smile.

Crystal cursed him for not giving his address and herself for not checking it in front of him. Now she would have to go a whole month with no contact and hope he stays true to his word. The tears returned again as she put the note back in her bag for safe keeping. If she could not communicate with him, at least she would have another piece of him to take with her. The rest of the afternoon passed as slow as any she had remembered. There was very little work for her to get through and she found herself for the most part simply watching the seconds drift by on the office clock, as well as thinking. Resigned to the fact she was no longer going to see Sean, at least not until she returned, all that was left was to resolve the problem that waited for her at home. There would need to be a clean break, but she could not see him out on the street. She would allow him to stay on in the house on the condition he was gone by the time she got back from her settling in period. She had made up her mind, that no matter what was to happen or what was to be said between now and Saturday, their relationship had reached its end.

The journey home was a pleasant one. Crystal had come to terms with Sean's decision to keep certain aspects of his life private, after all their friendship was still relatively young and she had accused him of being a stalker. The recollection of this fact along with *her* asking for *his* address made her chuckle. She had also come to terms, in her head anyway, that she was now relationship status, single. The sex was as perfect as his body, but the same old life routines he is so comfortable living out were becoming as uninteresting as his conversational skills. She could not help but begin to think, once she had let go of this anchor she could allow herself to drift towards that little piece of heaven she so longed for.

A little piece of her thought her man would be waiting on the platform, perhaps with some flowers and a huge apology. As the train pulled into the platform, that particular little thought was burst like a bubble. She made the short walk home, now contemplating the kind of reception she was to face there. As she turned the key in the lock a nervous uneasiness came over her. Something was not as it should be, and a lot of banging around only helped to confirm matters.

Entering the hallway, there was a note on the side unit simply marked 'Crystal'. She picked it up and read aloud, 'Thanks for the good times.' Putting it back calmly and walking to the stairs her man appeared at the top carrying a collection of bags and suitcase. 'That's all you were going to offer? After all we've been through and the time we've shared you were going to leave me a note with *thanks for the good times*! I know you say you're crap at confrontations but now you're taking the piss.' He began to walk down the stairs and offered timidly 'I didn't want to make things difficult.' Crystal allowed him to pass her in the hallway and followed him into the living room. 'So where are you going to stay?' she questioned. 'A friend from the gym is picking me up.' As if by brilliant timing a car horn outside suggested she had been within minutes of catching him before he had left for good.

'So who is it? Do I know them? It's another woman isn't it?' The silence that followed was all the confirmation she needed. 'So how long has it been going on?' she continued to press, as still he said nothing whilst making his way passed her into the hallway. 'So this is the end?' she asked knowing it was not really a question, not one she needed an answer too anyway. He opened the door and struggled with his bag towards the car. Crystal looked on in a combination of shock and horror as the driver got out. It was Jenny. For only the second time ever in her presence, she was not the bubbly ball of glee she was renown. Instead she kept her head low and made no attempt to look Crystal's way. 'You're leaving with her? The one who got herself fired for sleeping around the office!' He looked back and responded 'Please don't make a scene.' His plea was like a red rag to a bull and before slamming the door on them both she retorted angrily, 'You're welcome to him. You're both as shallow as a puddle.'

Crystal wept uncontrollably, finally allowing the tears she had fought so hard to conceal to now flow. The house felt very empty and she was alone. Even on those Sundays, when she would spend all day on her own, it had never felt this empty. There was an empty space under the TV where his games console used to live with the stack of games. It was the one thing she hadn't packed away. Walking upstairs she was aware that in order to fully take all his belongings, he would have had to have gone through all the already sealed boxes and cases. Sure enough, the bedroom was strewn with items now unpacked that weren't his or he didn't want. If it was possible for the tears to fall harder, they would have. With seeing him with Jenny and now seeing the state he was prepared to leave the house, any lingering love she had for the man had withered and died. Crystal threw herself on the bed and sobbed into her pillow.

The house was in darkness when Crystal opened her eyes, and it took a couple of moments for them to adjust. They were sore from all the tears she had shed, but looking at the alarm clock it confirmed that it was the early hours of the morning. Undressing from the previous day's work clothes she wrapped herself in a dressing gown and made her way downstairs. The house still felt empty without him but she kept telling herself that in a couple of days, she too would be gone. After fixing up a quick bite to eat, Crystal returned to her room and began sorting through the unpacked packing.

As the alarm sounded, Crystal was sat having already showered, dressed and rearranged everything to how she once had it having decided not to return to sleep. The agenda for the day was to keep busy and stop her mind from thinking about having lost two men in the space of a day. Although there was a chance to meet with Sean upon her return, the way her luck had been going, she thought it unlikely. Finishing off one of the many cups of coffee drunk since waking, she prepared to leave for her penultimate day in the office.

The walk to the station was pleasant in the early morning sun. Watching all the other people as they went about their business, Crystal wondered if they too ever had reasons to wish for something different. Were there others that wished to the powers that be for an escape from what their lives had become? Was she the only one to have fallen victim to the old saying 'be careful what you wish for'? As the train arrived to bringing her too her senses, 'so much for not dwelling on things' she thought. Seated on the train, Crystal decided it would be a good chance to again practice her Spanish. Again faces looked at her in amusement as the words stuttered from her lips. It was only when a small group of students started laughing at her hapless attempts she thought it best to stop to avoid further humiliation. The rest of the journey to the office was done in silence, but not before detouring for chocolate. Today was definitely another chocolate day.

The office fell silent as Crystal entered, a clear indication she was once again the centre of her colleagues gossip. 'You're all going to miss me when I'm gone. You'll need to find someone else to be the focus for your idle chatter' she offered to no one in particular. A voice from the back corner failed miserably in whispering 'I told you she didn't have friends in here.' Though it hurt her to hear it, the fact of the matter was, it was true. Despite talking with them on a work basis, she knew none of them away from the office. Perhaps if she did, she would have known Jenny attended the same gym as *him,* that she could drive and literally no man, or woman of that matter, were off limits. Returning to the attentions of work, she tried again to block it from her mind.

The rest of the day passed in fair nondescript fashion. Lunch came and went with only the odd jibe about not having anywhere to go. 'Maybe this is why we're not friends away from here' she thought, 'all the petty back biting and sarcasm gets tedious really quick.' By the time she was ready to leave, there were the odd few questions thrown her way about how she felt just having the one day left, but for the most part everyone went their own separate ways. Crystal walked to the station thinking of the empty house she was going to return home to, and could not help but think a delay to the trains would be welcome. Maybe she would have been better staying back at work at least there she would have had the cleaners for company. The train pulled in on time.

Crystal arrived home and instantly the feeling that it could no longer be called *home* descended upon her. Gone was the cosy feeling the heating gave her the first time she walked through the door. Gone was the unknowing of where *he* was and what he had been doing. What she was now standing in was a house. Any feeling of it being the home it used to be, walked out the door with him. All that was left here were the ghosts of memories they once shared.

After changing into her scruffs and raiding the cupboards for any comfort food she had left lying around, Crystal settled herself on the sofa and started to read her book of Spanish phrases. At least within the confines of these four walls, no-one was going to laugh and poke fun at her terrible pronunciation. It was also the first time in a while that conversation flowed during mealtime, albeit very one sided. When the time came and Crystal called an end to the evening, it was laying in bed alone that saw the tears return. 'Damn you genie' she shouted at the ceiling 'all I wished for was a little piece of Heaven, and instead I've been given Hell. Spain had better be the start of something wonderful.' She closed her eyes and waited for sleep.

For the second day running Crystal was up and ready before the alarm sounded. No matter how much she tried to suppress the thoughts in her head, they continued to fight against it and it was stopping her sleeping. It was beginning to show too as she felt lethargic and was filled with a *cant be arsed* attitude. All she wanted was for the day to be over with as quickly as possible. Thinking of everything she would need to do once she got home, there would be very little chance of an early night.

Despite her current mindset, Crystal had opted for a very calculated set of attire for her last day. Back came the high slit skirt and a rather see through floral blouse, under which she opted for a rather skimpy sexy set of lingerie. Today she did not care if people chose to stare in fact she wished they would. Anything to suggest she had not lost it when it came to being sexually attractive. There was one thing being in control of ending a relationship, but seeing the one you end it with leave with a younger more nubile version, does very little for the self esteem.

Crystal had never counted the steps taken to reach the station, deeming it too far and also too early in the day. In an attempt to break her lethargy and *cba* attitude she began. After three thousand, six hundred and twenty three steps, several wolf whistles and copious amounts of returned smiles, she reached the station. 'That won't be something I'll do again' she said to herself. The train was already on the platform and it meant a dash to catch the doors before they closed. Whilst she had mastered the art of walking in heels, running she had not. With the elegance and grace of a drunk on ice, she tumbled into the carriage with arms and legs flailing.

Several of the other passengers helped her to a seat, where she sat red in the face and too embarrassed to look at any one. After several minutes, and when a seat was available, an older lady moved to sit near her. 'Can I give you some words of wisdom my dear?' she asked. Crystal agreed fearing the worst. 'Every woman should choose shoes she can run in. Be that either for a train or bus, or from possible danger. Meaning no disrespect, dressed as you are and based on your attempts at the first scenario, I fear for you should you ever face the second.' Flashbacks of the poor girl attacked in her street came crashing back to her. Crystal looked at her beautiful high heels and then at the canvas slipons of her older fellow commuter. She was right of course, but they would never have gone with her outfit.

One thousand, seven hundred and forty three steps, same as it always had been. This was going to be the last time she would walk through this door before heading off for her four weeks in the sun, and upon entering the office her colleagues were aware of this fact also. They had gathered around her desk with a beautiful bunch of flowers and a wonderfully chocolaty looking cake. There was a small ripple of applause as she made her way to her desk, clearly overwhelmed by the fuss made. 'Thank you, all of you. I am deeply touched.' Crystal said to the small gathering fighting back any tears. She had cried so much of late, even though these were of joy, they were not welcome.

The thing about life is that any distractions from the normal routine are often short lived. This was no more evident than, having been sat at her desk a matter of minutes, the whole office quickly returned to its usual daily schedule. Despite a brief interlude discussing plans for tomorrow with Mr Hines, the day had quickly moved on to lunch. The cake was exceedingly delicious and was received by one and all in the office without refusal, much to Crystal's disappointment, as she had eyed any leftover pieces for her tea that evening. 'Probably just as well if I want to get into my swim suit' she thought.

As the afternoon went on, Crystal could not help but think about how she was going to say goodbye to everyone. It was funny how she was only going for a month, and yet it seemed as though it would be the last time she saw them. With her *to do* tray empty and all the final plans sorted, she was ready for home. After one last meeting with boss, one by one she walked around the office and said her farewell. Where Crystal had expected tears, a smile graced her face at the realisation she was on the cusp of something new. Something that was sure to break all her current routines.

Making her way home Crystal stopped at every opportunity to take in the sights and sounds around her. She wondered just how much all the familiar sights will have changed a month from now. There was a beauty to be found if you knew where and looked hard enough, something she had not done too often. The question was, was this beauty one she would be grateful to see after four weeks away? Standing outside her door, she sighed heavily and braced herself for a night of last minute chores and packing before her taxi came to take her away. 'This is it Crystal' she said to herself 'the last night before the rest of your life.'

The door opened and Crystal dropped her bag in complete shock as she was confronted with 'Hi babe!' *It was him*, bold as brass standing in the hallway awaiting her return. 'Kept a key then I see' she said bending down to pick up her belongings that had fallen out her bag. 'Kindly put it on the side and close the door behind you when you leave' she continued. He held out a hand to help her up, but she ignored it instead opting for the door frame for support. 'You look nice' he offered as she passed him on her way to the kitchen. 'You didn't come here to tell me I looked *nice* now did you? What do you want?' He joined her in the kitchen and attempted to put on the charm he knew had worked so many times in the past, 'I'd like us to try again. Being apart has shown me just how much I miss you.' Crystal looked at him sceptically, 'and?' she asked. There was a pause as anyone could see he was scrambling for the right answer. Eventually he murmured 'I want you to stay' A pan whizzed very close to his head as Crystal raged at him to leave. 'I love you' he said timidly ducking and moving back into the hallway. 'YOU want ME to stay? What about what I want? As for you love me! I doubt very much if you are capable of love.' Another pan flew towards his head. He pleaded desperately making his way through the front door, 'Crystal, baby. I love you!' Slamming the door in his face she shouted after him, 'But I no longer love you.'

Saying those words lifted a heavy weight from her heart. Crystal had never doubted her love for him was real and that she was not in fact blinded by infatuation, but once she could see the grim reality that he so ready to just walk away the last embers of that love faded to just a whisper of smoke. 'Emergency locksmith' she thought as she started on the last of the chores, 'seems he's over his confrontation issues too.' By the time she was fully ready to leave, and in possession of a new full set of keys, the night was turning to morning. Crystal bedded down setting the alarm for an hour before her taxi and closed her eyes for a final time before Spain.

Crystal woke on the sound of the alarm. There was a spring in her step and renewed enthusiasm to her *get up and go*. She showered and dressed in a beautiful free flowing floral dress and matched it with a bolero cardigan and wedge shoes. Already she was feeling in the mood for feeling the Spanish sun on her skin. With one final check around the place, she opened the door to the taxi driver who had just knocked and helped him load her cases into the boot. Locking the door behind her, she jumped into the car and they pulled away. 'Going anywhere nice' the driver asked inquisitively. 'To find a little slice of heaven' she replied gazing out the window.

Crystal sat in the airport waiting for her boarding gate to be called. It seemed as though she had been waiting hours, such was the level of boredom that had begun to set in. She had never been one for people watching, but with the varied walks of life that she was to share a plane with, she could not her herself staring. There were the business men in their shirt and tie, no doubt flying first or business class at their company's expense. The holiday makers with their overly excited hyper children who insisted on ignoring their pleas to stop running around, then you had the young lovers, always draped over each other and the excessive use of public displays of affection. With a two hour flight ahead of her, Crystal cringed at the thought of being sat next to any of them. Especially given that she was going to be flying economy at the expense of her company.

As the passengers boarded the plane and found their seats, she took her place next to the window. 'At least I can stare at the clouds if the company proves to be annoying' she thought just as a young woman took her seat beside her. She was quite clearly nervous and offered a timid greeting as Crystal turned to face her. 'Is this your first time flying?' she asked. The young woman nodded as the colour visibly drained from her cheeks. 'This is going to be a long two hours' she thought watching as the young woman reached for the paper bag in front of her.

The remaining seat in their group of three was taken by an older man. He was dressed in thick corduroy trousers matched with a shirt and woolly jumper. Crystal could not help but think the poor man was going to be in for a shock when they depart the plane into the hot Spanish sun. 'Good morning' she offered with a smile. 'Well aren't I the lucky one, being put next to two rather fine looking ladies?' Her smile remained until she gradually moved her gaze back to the window. Conversation continued without her involvement and focused on the young woman's increasing sickness towards flying. 'It's only two hours' Crystal muttered under her breath.

'Well that was two hours of my life I'm never getting back' was Crystal's response as the plane touched down. In between stories of family emigrating from *good old Blighty,* and the constant vomiting it had been the flight from Hell. The in flight movie was one she had seen before and whatever it was they were calling food was made inedible by the poor woman's sickness. Thankfully though she was just minutes away from feeling the sun on her skin and meeting once again that fine specimen of a man Mr Munoz. The smile had returned to Crystal's face once more.

With the formalities complete and her luggage collected, she was very surprised to see that it was in fact

Mr Lavkin that stood waiting for her. 'Afternoon Crystal, I hope you had a pleasant flight?' he asked whilst taking her case from her. 'It was very pleasant indeed thank you Mr Lavkin.' He looked at her and smiled, 'Please call me David. After all, we are not in work now.' She smiled and followed him from the airport to where he had parked. 'Thank you David. No Mr Munoz then?' Opening the car door for her, he waited till he too was inside before answering. 'Sadly no, he will be meeting us there. The natives, how shall I put it, are a little restless?'

Their destination was a small market town on the edge of the Alboran Sea, about an hour drive from the airport. The scenery alone was enough to take Crystals breathe away, starting the journey passing along the side of some beautiful rolling mountains. 'Part of the National Park' David informed her noticing she had not stopped staring out of the window the whole time. 'It's beautiful.' The further they drove, the more the scenery turned more rural and before too long the sea came into view. 'Now *that* is beautiful' David remarked. 'But it's just, well a bit, barren!' Crystal offered with a tinge of scepticism. 'Exactly, now imagine it all bought by us and then transformed into a holiday haven.' She could almost imagine him counting the pounds in his mind whilst she could not help but think that this was very much a case of *all been done before* and on a much larger scale.

'Here we are, Ramón's home.' Crystal stared at the farmhouse at the end of a dusty track. 'Not what I was expecting at all' she murmured with more than a hint of disappointment. 'It better have a pool'. As they pulled up outside, Mr Munoz came to greet them, closely followed by a younger looking woman. 'I trust you had a pleasant journey? Come, we have prepared some food.' Crystal found herself staring at this beautiful woman and thinking 'Why did she have to be so damn good looking?' The decor inside was minimalistic, yet rustic adorned with lots of wood and ceramics. This was a home with a definite woman's touch. The table displayed various plates of cooked fish that had no doubt been caught locally, green salad cheeses and breads. There was wine by the bottle and it all looked far and away more appetising than that served to her on the plane. 'La Comida?' Crystal offered gingerly. 'Bien hecho. Someone has been practicing I see. Eat and drink, and once you are done we shall show you to your room for siesta' replied Ramón with a smile.

   With everyone seated and thoroughly enjoy the banquet of food before them, Crystal could not help but think that *this* was exactly what meal times should be like. There were no awkward silences as everybody offered something to the conversation. The focus though was mainly about her and what she had expected making the commitment to move to Spain. It was just like being back in the office instead here the gossip was in the form of questions asked directly to her. Attempting to deflect the attention, Crystal moved the conversation to work. 'Mr Lavkin, sorry, David said' noticing his raised eyebrow 'something about the locals being a little restless?' Ramón finished what he was eating as all eyes were on him for a response, 'It would appear some of the local people are, how do you say, not keen to see things change.' Mrs Munoz gave a displeasing look and offered reason as if speaking for the community, 'Ramón, these are simple people. Generations have grown and worked these lands and you would have them sell it all for a few coins so that you can build your hotels and parks. These are the people who took you as one of their own.'

It was Mr Lavkin who broke the conversation before it went down avenues best not ventured. 'Well I'm about ready for that siesta now. That was a glorious spread of food again Catalina, very tasty as always.' He turned his attention to Crystal and offered to carry her luggage. 'You stay here too?' she asked looking puzzled. 'Where else would I be staying?' he replied laughing, 'There are no hotels yet.'

The two respectfully excused themselves from the table and made their way down the hall towards the back of the house. Crystal could hear the conversation resume between Ramón and his wife in their native tongue as soon as they were out of sight. She looked towards David who simply shrugged and continued on towards her room. It was compact with just a bed, a bedside cabinet and wardrobe inside. There was also a small window that stopped it feeling like a prison cell. 'It's not much, but you get used to it. I'll leave you to your rest.' Crystal thanked him as he put down her bags and closed the door as he left. 'What have you got yourself into Crystal' she said sitting on the bed and looking around the room. This was not the heaven she had imagined earlier that morning.

Crystal tried in vain to fall asleep, despite the idea of an afternoon nap being a pleasurable one. There was too much going on in her head and so whilst the rest of the house was quiet, she opted for a walk so as to take in more of her new surroundings. She had noticed the small town down by the sea on her approach to the farm, easily within walking distance and would provide an ideal chance to get to know what the place had to offer. Leaving the Munoz family home, there was no sign of the pool she had wished for.

'One, two, three' she counted under her breathe with every stride as she made her way along the road into town. 'Nine thousand, three hundred and fourteen and that brings me to the edge of town.' Crystal gazed around at the sorry looking white buildings that had once seen better days. The occasional splatter of colour from potted flowers helped to lift the ambience of the place, but it felt tired and sleepy. Even with the time for siesta over, the few people she saw did not exactly do much and what they did was with no real urgency. Walking further around the few streets in town, it was clear in her mind why her company had chosen this place for re-development, although it seemed such a shame to want to destroy the tranquillity for the hustle and bustle of budget tourism. It was no wonder those that lived here were so opposed to their plans.

'You are English, no?' came an elderly male voice behind her. Crystal spun to see who it was only to see a figure step inside a nearby home. 'You are not welcome.' added the old man as he disappeared from view. 'I'm beginning to wish I wasn't here' she said to herself, deciding it was probably best to head back to the farm. 'Not that there is any better.' The thought of four weeks may as well have been a lifetime, with the prospect of having to mediate between the local community and her bosses being the nail to seal the coffin. Perhaps if she detached any emotional sentiment from what was required of her, the time would pass quickly and she could get herself back on the plane.

Catalina was the first she saw as she approached the farm. 'Crystal, I was just looking for you. Have you just been into the town?' Crystal nodded. 'Yes, although I'm not sure I was that welcome.' Catalina waited upon her to come closer and spoke much more quietly as if only to be heard by the two of them, 'You are a very lovely woman. Do not get dragged in to affairs here. My advice would be to not stay and have the conscience of what happens here live with you. The families that live here have done so for many generations and will not move easily. Do not be a part of destroying my home.' Crystal looked deep within the anguish contained in Catalina's eyes, then looked towards the town she had just visited. Heaven it seems takes on many guises and can be found almost anywhere.

Crystal made her way to her room, passing Ramón and David on the way. They were laughing about the spot they were standing would soon be one of the holes on the planned golf course, David even pretending to swing an imaginary club. She sighed deeply and closed the door to her room. Never before had she faced such guilt about what she did for a living. Back home she moved around empty property from business to business as they became available. Sure it involved peoples' livelihoods falling on hard times and them having to close, but never did she come face to face with them. Here she was expected to play with peoples' lives, their ancestry, their very way of life. The burden sat heavy on her conscience, especially more so knowing Catalina opposed her husband and that he himself planned to sell their own family home from under them. Crystal sat on the bed and tried to rationalise the situation she found herself in.

A knock on the door woke Crystal from the slumber she had just slipped into. Before she was able to acknowledge who it was that woke her, the door opened. It was Ramón. He stood reminiscent of some god like statue staring at her, motionless as if in awe of what was before him. She stood from the bed and made her way over to him, reaching out and placing her hand upon his chest. It was solid to the touch, yet she could feel his heart beating fast and heavy. Crystal looked deep into his eyes as she began to unbutton his shirt so as to touch is muscled dark olive skin, inhaling deep to take in his scent. Another knock on the door shattered the illusion.

'It was a dream? I might have known' she said to herself with a tinge of resignation 'at least it wasn't David'. A sudden bolt of realisation hit her like a hammer. 'I'm here again. David is Sean, carrying my bags and opening car doors and being the perfect gentleman. Ramón is that cheating scumbag of an ex boyfriend. All body beautiful sleeping with an equally good looking woman.' Crystal suddenly felt an edge of guilt over her last comment, based on the fact he was not cheating on her with Catalina, and the fact she actually seemed a really nice person. Another knock on the door prompted her to this time open it. David stood waiting patiently ready to inform her that food was being prepared if she cared to join them.

'Ramón and Catalina, are they married?' Crystal enquired as they made their way towards the kitchen. 'Oh yes, for several years now. I believe once the development goes through, Ramón is keen to have children.' He was becoming less like the man she said goodbye to more and more. 'He is beautiful' she said wistfully. 'Yes she is isn't she? You did say *she* didn't you?' Crystal laughed as they entered the kitchen, neither confirming nor denying his question. 'What is so funny?' asked Ramón inquisitively. David looked at the way a sparkle flared in Crystal's eyes the moment she saw *him*. 'Oh just a little clarity on a situation' he replied as he offered her a seat at the table.

The main meal was much smaller than that which greeted her during lunch. A selection of chicken pieces on a bed of green salad was accompanied by rice and a tomato dressing. Catalina had worked her magic in the kitchen again. 'I hear you explored the town earlier?' Ramón asked smiling as he did so. 'I hope you did not fall in love with it' he laughed. Crystal could not decide if he was indeed making a joke, or being sarcastically serious. 'Actually I found the place to have an air of peace and tranquillity seldom found these days.' An awkward silence fell around the table. 'Okay he was being serious' she thought as she turned her attention to the meal. Crystal could not help but notice the smile being offered to her from Catalina since her comments. Smiling back she recalled the conversation they both had earlier in the day.

David turned his attention to Crystal, 'You are still focused on assisting us in seeing out the company vision aren't you?' She scrambled for the words to say, frantically looking at Catalina for help. 'Erm, whilst I can see why our company has plans for this place. Erm, there is part of me that thinks it's a shame.' Ramón stood so as to impose more authority on proceedings. 'It's a shame?' he started mockingly, 'We will put this place on the map. Generate more money from the land than these people have ever dreamed of seeing from it.' Catalina took her husband by the arm. 'And you! You were the one who always complained about being bored, wanting more from life other than that passed to you by your mother. We are offering you *more* and yet you oppose that which *you* wish for.' Ramón left the room in a rage as Catalina stood to go after him. 'I'll go!' offered David, 'See if I can't calm that Spanish temper of his.'

'Gracias Crystal, but you did not have to speak out. Now you will be forever in trouble with David and Ramón.' Crystal wryly smiled and moved seats so as the two could talk with a degree of privacy. 'I was once like you. Bored of how my life was the same thing day after day. Then I met a man who was different to the one I was with.' Catalina interjected puzzled, 'You were, unfaithful?' 'No, no. We were, *are* friends. He was that something different that was missing in my life. I thought coming here was, but now I see this was a mistake.' Crystal drifted off in lost thought. 'You left them both behind?' Catalina pressed further. 'No, just the one. The important one.'

David returned alone and sat with the two women. Catalina looked at him for a measure of her husband's mood. 'He is very passionate about seeing this venture succeed that is all' he offered. Crystal looked and Catalina and she in turn to Crystal. 'David, I will be returning home on the next available flight. I came here hoping to get involved in something I could feel passionate about, something I could throw myself into. None one told me those that lived here were opposed to your plans and I can see why they are.' Ramón had arrived at the door to overhear of her plans. 'Crystal, you came here as our guest first and an employee to company second. I respect your decision if not your reasons, but please, stay awhile longer before you return home.' He joined the others in sitting at the table and poured a glass of wine, offering it to Crystal. 'Come, let us forget talk of work and enjoy the evening as friends.'

As the wine continued to flow and evening became early morning, the events of the day began to take its toll on Crystal. Retiring respectfully, she made her way to her room very aware that in her absence talk would now turn to her sudden change of heart. She hoped that her tiredness would send her to sleep and that her mind would be willing to allow it also. Entering her room she could just hear David say, 'perhaps letting her know all the facts before she came would have been better.' Crystal tutted as the door closed preventing any more of the conversation from being heard. After readying herself for turning in, she switched off the light signalling an end to a hectic first day.

The morning had almost slipped Crystal by when she finally awoke. Catalina was busy with her chores and there was no sign of the two men. 'Did we sleep well? We knocked upon your door, but when you did not answer we assumed you needed more rest. There is coffee in the pot, or fresh orange in the fridge. Please, help yourself.' Crystal made her way into the kitchen, 'I think yesterday must have taken it out of me. I can't remember the last time I slept so late.' Catalina followed so as to fill the mop bucket she was carrying. 'Well you did have quite the eventful day. Are you still planning on returning home? You know you are more than welcome to stay as long as you like.' Crystal smiled and poured herself a mug of strong black coffee. 'This isn't where I'm meant to be Catalina. I was fooling myself into believing that coming here would be the big change my life needed, and in a way it was. Had I not come I would still be blindly devoted to the one I thought I loved, still be doing a job I neither liked nor loathed.' Catalina turned with the bucket now full and mop in hand, 'and you left behind someone special.' Crystal smiled in a way as to acknowledge the statement as fact.

The men had gone off early to fish and would be gone most of the day. Catalina continued with cleaning an already spotless home and so Crystal decided to repay the hospitality shown to her by preparing the evening meal. There were no prepacked frozen foods, just good wholesome freshly grown produce. It was something she had missed with her busy lifestyle, and relished the chance to prepare a meal from scratch as she had done under the guidance of her mother. 'Wow has it been that long ago!' she mused now hoping Catalina would not be too critical of her efforts in her kitchen.

She decided to opt for a more English feel to her chosen meal, serving lamb with roast potatoes and assorted vegetables, even trying her hand at a stewed fruit crumble. Everything was ready and the table set, but there was still no sign of Ramón and David. 'Catalina. What time do they normally return home?' she asked pacing around the kitchen watching over the food. 'Who knows when it comes to men? Will it not keep till they do?' Crystal sighed, wishing perhaps she had started when she knew they were home. 'Not really. It should really be eaten now. A tear started form in the corner of her eye at the fear of her efforts going to waste, her voice showing of her disappointment also. Whilst it may have been something a little different for Ramón and Catalina, she had hoped David may have appreciated the little slice of home on a plate. Crystal plated up four portions, placed them on the table and waited.

Several hours had passed before the two finally returned from their day out on the boat. Catalina and Crystal had tried in vain to salvage as much of the meal as possible but there was very little still edible from the original meal. David was first to offer some condolence at having missed Crystal's efforts, Ramón on the other hand was not so diplomatic, 'Perhaps a book on our culture would have been better than on our language.' Crystal snapped back without care for offending the master of the house, 'Perhaps if I was staying and you were not planning on destroying the very culture of the place, then I may have been open to learn. Perhaps you should start learning that of those you wish to attract.' She stormed out of the kitchen and to her room hearing Ramón remonstrating about being spoken to the way he had. Crystal slammed the door behind her and wondered, 'Why all good looking men such arseholes?'

Having decided that this would be her last night under the same roof as *that* man, Crystal began to pack her belongings. Come Hell or high water, she was going to be on a plane back home to England at some point tomorrow. There was a knock on the door followed by David's calm and sincere voice, 'Crystal, may I come in?' Begrudgingly she agreed and he joined her with a plate of food Catalina had prepared for her. 'She thought you may have been hungry' he said laying the plate down on the bedside unit. 'I don't suppose there is any point in me trying to convince you to stay?' She gave him a look that suggested his question was both stupid and needed no answer. 'Then I shall drive you to the airport first thing and assist you in securing a flight home. You are aware that I will have to contact Mr Hines and let him know?' Crystal stopped packing briefly and thought long and hard about what she was going to say next.

David left her to her packing and closed the door as he went. She looked at the plate he had brought in to see that it was. Slices of chorizo and small fried eggs sat on pieces of toasted bread, and she had to admit it looked rather tasty, even if it was not the Sunday roast she had planned to be sitting down to. There were no doubt other servings to be had, but she could not bring herself to join them in light of her outburst. Crystal finished that which was on her plate and returned to her packing constantly mulling over the thought of having to walk back into her old office, suffer the whispers and assumptions from her old colleagues, not to mention telling Mr Hines that which she told David just moments ago. There was no doubting that sleep was going to be hard to come by this evening.

Catalina was the next to visit. She did so under the guise of collecting the empty plate and seeing if she could bring her anything further to eat or drink. Noticing the packed bags at the end of the bed she asked if her leaving so soon was as a result of her altercation with Ramón. 'We both know I was planning on returning home, tonight just brought that plan a little closer.' Crystal explained. 'It would have been nice having another female around for a bit longer.' Said Catalina picking up the plate 'especially one who shares views as I do.' Crystal mustered a smile 'I've enjoyed the time we've spent together, albeit short. I'm sure if you fight hard enough, you too will find your little slice of heaven as I'm sure I will.' Catalina smiled back opening the door to leave, 'I am sure you are right. Sleep well.' With the door closed, Crystal laid herself on the bed and closed her eyes.

The morning arrived to find Crystal busy in the kitchen. She had prepared a good selection of pancakes and fresh orange for everyone as a parting gift and by way of making up for the failed attempts in the kitchen yesterday. Catalina and David graciously sat to sample morning offering, Ramón on the other hand ignored the spread and without even acknowledging her presence he made his way out of the house. 'Good morning Ramón. Yes I slept very well thank you' Crystal sniped after him. 'Perhaps we should get you away sooner rather than later' remarked David helping himself to several of the sweeter pancakes on the table. 'I am ready when you are' she replied. Catalina sat in silence.

David brought Crystal's bag through to the kitchen ready to put into the car. She was in the process of saying her goodbyes to Catalina and sharing in the shedding of the odd tear and parting hug. 'I hope you continue to fight. This place is beautiful and deserves to be kept so.' Catalina smiled at her words. 'And you return home and let him know how important he is.' Crystal could not help but laugh and agree, turning to help David with her bags. Much to Crystal's disappointment there was no sign of Ramón. Despite their little altercation, it would have been nice to have left at least saying goodbye. David held the car door open and waited for her.

The drive to the airport seemed to take for ages, certainly a lot longer than the hour that passed would suggest. The scenery that captivated her on her arrival now did little to hold her attention. David's attempts to break the journey with conversation almost fell upon deaf ears. Crystal's mind was elsewhere. 'So what will you do when you get home?' he asked, 'Do you have food in? Looking forward to being in your own bed?' Crystal looked at him blankly, 'Sorry, have I been ignoring you?' He gave a little laugh, 'It's fine. I understand you have a lot on your mind.' She turned her attention back to just staring out of the window. 'You have no idea!'

When they eventually arrived at the airport David insisting on getting the door and helping her with the luggage. 'A gentleman to the end' Crystal complimented on his impeccable conduct. 'There is no price for good manners, and it's for that reason I am obligated to ring Rupert once you're on the plane.' The confused look on her face prompted him to explain further, 'Mr Hines! To let him know you are returning.' All Crystal could say was 'Rupert!' David gave her that look, like a parent would to a child misbehaving, 'Yes, Rupert Hines, though he seldom likes to be called by his first name. Come on, we have a ticket to buy.' She could not help but laugh like a mischievous child, "Rupert!"

With ticket in hand and luggage away on the conveyor, Crystal turned to David to offer a goodbye, 'I'm sorry I wasted everybody's time.' He looked at the disappointment in her eyes, 'Would you have come if we had been honest with you from the start?' he asked. 'Probably not' she answered with a sympathetic tone. 'Then we probably did right in taking the chance once you were here. Do not fret. You concentrate on finding that which makes you happy.' He held out his hand, but she ignored it instead opting to throw her arms round him. 'Thank you' she whispered then released her hold on him. 'Say *I'm sorry* to Ramón for me.' David waved her away 'Go! Get your plane before you're stuck here.' She turned and headed away. Turning back one last time, he continued to watch her off waving her away further with a smile.

Sitting in the airport lounge, Crystal could feel an air of relief knowing that within a couple of hours she would be walking through her own front door, jump into her bed and not have to be answerable to anyone. Certainly looking at the others waiting to board it appeared that her feelings were shared amongst a number of her fellow travellers. There is definitely something magical about returning home after being away, no matter how short. Her only concern would be that it did indeed feel like home, and not just the four walls it did when she left. One thing was certain, she was about to start another new chapter in her search for happiness.

The flight was long and arduous. She found herself sandwiched between an elderly woman who insisted on trying to share her sweets whilst telling her all about her holiday, and a young man who had spend the last few years backpacking in an attempt to *find himself*. What passed as food was as bad as she remembered from the last time. Catalina's home fresh home cooking was definitely going to be missed, even the boiled sweets the old woman was offering had more edible appeal. The young man beside her had noticing that it was going to be left looked at her and enquired 'May I?' Crystal could only assume his taste for food had been destroyed with whatever he had been eating on his years travelling. 'Be my guest' she replied handing him the plate. Crystal reclined in her seat the best she could and tried to sleep.

Making her way through the airport arrivals lounge, Crystal looked out at the typical rainy English weather. There was a certain degree of comfort she found in the predictability of it. With luggage collected she made her way to find a taxi that would take her home. She could not wait to start making the required changes she had planned in order to make the place her own again. If moving away was not the answer, then perhaps altering familiar surrounding could be. One thing was for certain, she had no intention of slipping back into the life she left behind only a couple of days ago.

The taxi pulled up outside her house and Crystal took a moment before leaving the car. The driver unloaded he bags and put them by her door for her before asking if she okay. 'I'm fine, it's just going to be a little weird going back through that door.' She paid the fare and continued to stare at the door whilst the taxi drove off. 'Well I'm going to have to do it eventually' she muttered as she put the key in the door. It was cold inside and dragging the bags into the hallway, Crystal realised that it still lacked the feeling of home. Crystal made her way around the living room and into the kitchen. 'Best do some shopping too' she said remembering she emptied all the cupboards and fridge before leaving. Turning back on the central heating Crystal left the bags in the hall and left for the shops hoping that when she returned, not only would the place feel warmer due to the heat, but also warmer in the homely sense.

The whole change started with the shopping. Gone was the convenience food that would have once filled her basket, instead ingredients that would allow her to experiment in creating the wonderful dishes as she remembered Catalina doing. Never before had she given food the love and care it deserved, and so now she found herself spending her time examining the quality of the produce as opposed to the time needed to cook. Suitably stocked, she made her way home to a house that had warmed beautifully. Crystal continued to ignore the cases, instead opting to set about dabbling with the food she had bought. It may not have been up to Catalina's culinary standard, but the results were tasty and the satisfaction of having made it from scratch pleased her greatly. If she could find as much enjoyment in pursuing her other planned changes, then maybe, just maybe, then that little slice of heaven she had so craved would be found.

Upstairs were still all the sealed boxes, those that were to be delivered to Spain and those heading to charity. Crystal decided to stick with the plan and phoned around in order to arrange collection for the later. If she was willing to see the stuff go before, she saw no reason to keep hold now. Even some of the stuff intended to be kept fell victim to the new ruthless Crystal, such was her desire to start afresh and say goodbye to the past. By the time the knock on the door came, eighty percent of her belongings were ready to find new homes. Once they had gone, it felt like eighty percent of the ghosts the house held had also been laid to rest. Crystal sat back against the bed feeling thoroughly satisfied with the outcome of having been so ruthless.

For the rest of the day Crystal opted for the more gentile approach of relaxing on the sofa with a glass of wine and a good book. There was no TV noise in the background, or the sound of that annoying games console. In fact there was no noise at all, it was perfect. The night drew in and still she sat in a blissful state lost in the words she was reading, oblivious to the fact she had not eaten anything substantial since getting back from the shops. As tiredness crept in, and her bed seemed a welcome retreat, the realisation of not only was she now hungry, but that tomorrow would bring the dreaded commute to work. Crystal rustled up another tasty bite to eat along with a mug of hot milk and retired upstairs to bed. Going back to the office to confront Rupert and the rest of her colleagues was going to demand of her all the patience and self confidence she could muster.

Crystal woke on the chimes of seven, dragged herself out of bed and proceeded to the shower. Feeling now more awake and refreshed, a chosen outfit of trouser suit and blouse was adorned. 'Best look respectable if I am to face the firing squad' she thought heading downstairs to fix breakfast. One cup of coffee and a slice of toast later and she was ready to take the short walk up to the station. The rain of yesterday had eased leaving behind an overcast but dry start to the day. Although Crystal had made this particular journey so many times in the past, something today felt very different. Even the *run the gauntlet* train journey lacked any of its usual haphazard craziness that would normally accompany her into work. It was the last part of the commute, those one thousand, seven hundred and forty three steps that brought the butterflies. The calm before the storm was over and now, stood in front of the door to the office and sense of déjà vu washed over her as she took in a deep breath and reached for the handle.

Sure enough, as she entered she was greeted by a throng of familiar faces all awash with a look of genuine astonishment. The whispers started almost immediately, followed by the comments about getting lost and not working there anymore. Crystal ignored them all and made her way to the door of Mr Hines' office. She knocked once and awaited a reply. 'Come in' came a voice from the other side. 'I must not call him Rupert.' she thought opening the door. Mr Hines was not at all surprised to see her, instead he simply gestured for her to take a seat. Crystal sat with a tremendous churning in the pit of her stomach preventing her from doing so comfortably. Nervously she fired the first salvo in what was to be a short battle of words. 'I quit! I'm sorry I wasted everyone's time, but I no longer wish to work in this field of business.' The words completely took the wind from the sails of her boss, as now he looked shocked. 'I'm guessing this is something you've been thinking about? Not just a knee jerk reaction to recent events?' Crystal stood and replied in doing so, 'Thinking about it yes, knee jerk no.' Rupert stood so as to be on equal footing and walked around his desk to cut off any hasty escape. 'And there is no way of making you change your mind? Crystal, you are good at your job and right, yes we were unhappy with what happened, but there is no escaping the fact if you left, we would be losing a great asset to the company.' The kind words were not lost on her as she smiled and opened the office door, but they did nothing to deter her from her decision. 'Very kind words indeed. Thank you, but I still quit.'

Another decision she had made was to not get bogged down in goodbyes. They had already said them when first she left that Friday gone, and so a bold statement of intent would be to just walk straight out. Mr Hines followed her out of his office and watched as she made her way to the main door. 'If you change your mind you know where we are.' He called out after her. Crystal raised her hand and waved goodbye without looking back. 'I won't' she replied leaving the building. As the door closed behind her she stopped and took in a deep breath of fresh air. The churning in her stomach had stopped and the butterflies flown away as she now knew these were the changes she needed in her life. The realisation of such put a massive smile on her face and filled her with renewed purpose.

It was the first time in as long as she could remember that she felt free. Sure there would be the need to find a new job so that bills got paid, but right here and now it felt as though the last of the shackles that were binding her to the lifestyle she so badly wanted to change from had been broken. With her new found freedom, Crystal set off to partake in a little retail indulgence, or at least window shop. She may have found herself with an abundance of free time, but sadly no abundance of free money. Her first stop, the little old book shop for some bargain buys so as to lose herself on the countless nights of reading she could now enjoy.

The smell of the books teased her senses just as the smell of Catalina's cooking had the first time she arrived at her home. The scent to Crystal was as homely and reassuring as that of freshly cooked pastries to others. The sight of the boxes unexplored and rammed with books of all shapes and sizes were enough to drive her into a near ecstatic state of bliss. The shop owner tutted loudly and mumbled something incomprehensible at the sight of his boxes being emptied, each book individually thumbed through, and then returned. Crystal sat and continued the same methodical process for hours, slowly build in pile of books she was intent on purchasing. 'I am guessing you *really* love your books' the owner finally asked having witnessed over a dozen boxes unpacked and repacked. 'There is nothing better than losing yourself in a story that someone has painstakingly devised and written for the pleasure of its readers. You know you could probably do with putting a lot of this stuff on display, they're kind of lost in these boxes.' The owner tutted again and shook his head. 'And just who is going to spend their time going through it all, separating it into genres and fighting with the cramped space we have? I myself have long lost the passion and inclination to keep up with it all.'

Sean's words rung loud in her ears, as if he himself were standing next to her shouting. 'Accept being poor if it means following your dreams.' Crystal stood up from where she had been sat amongst the books. 'I'll gladly do it, if you have a job vacancy!' she offered eagerly. The owner laughed and pointed out the high volume of customers coming in and out. 'I don't earn enough for two wages, only just enough to warrant keeping this place open. What are there, roughly ten thousand books in here? Priced at roughly a pound each? You bring me enough to buy all the books in here, and I'll give it all to you and gladly sign over the lease. Though I doubt someone a smart as you would be so bold or foolish.' Crystal could hardly contain the excitement building within, 'Call me a fool if you will, but if you're true to your word, then I will indeed buy all this from you.' The two shook hands as if to form a binding contract all the while Crystal giggling like an over excited child. The opportunity to own her favourite shop was more than any dream she could have ever wished to have come true. The only challenge now was getting her hands on the ten thousand pounds needed to tie up the deal. Crystal picked up the books she had put aside for buying and handed them over to the owner. 'I make that twelve pound altogether, so shall I knock that from your ten thousand pound valuation?' They both shared in a laugh before she left.

Crystal knew that without a job it was going to be hard to convince any bank to loan her the money. She could return to Mr Hines with her tail between her legs and grovel for her old job back so as to fund any loan, but having freed the shackles, she was reluctant to see put back on. Her only realistic option was to offer her home as collateral, although the thought of risking the roof over her head scared her greatly, especially given that it had again started to feel like home. Sean's words rang loud once again in her ears and she knew that if she was to find the happiness she wanted, then risks would have to be taken. Already she had taken so many that a few more could not hurt. 'Besides,' she said to herself, 'If it all starts to fall apart, *then* I'll swallow my pride and go back.'

After spending several minutes in her local bank, a meeting was arranged for the following morning. 'If everything is in order, then you should have the money in your account shortly after the meeting' the young woman at the counter confirmed. Crystal left with a sense of nervous excitement and decided it time to head home having had way too much happen to her today already. The train was busy with no seating to be had being full of those finishing work or returning home from a day shopping. 'Standing room only then I see' she exclaimed climbing on board. 'You didn't expect to find chivalry on here did you?' a woman much older than her asked as if to highlight the fact she too had to stand. 'Oh I found it once, but it must have been from a real man. Not many of those around anymore though' Crystal expressed loud enough for all to hear. It fell upon deaf ears as no one budged from their coveted seats.

Having finally made it home, she put her books to one side for reading later and made her way upstairs to slip into something more comfortable. She sat on the bed and again reflected upon the massive decisions she had made and how it was going to impact on her life. Self-doubt began to creep in as she questioned whether or not she was doing the right thing, even though she could also hear the clichés about *never knowing till you try* and *regret not trying is worse than regret failing*. One thing she knew with absolute certainty though was with all that had happened today she was now feeling rather peckish. Crystal stood and made her way downstairs to the kitchen with her mind set on trying to replicate the chorizo, egg and toast Catalina had brought to her. The result was something similar and just as satisfying.

For the rest of the evening Crystal indulged in throwing herself into her reading. It was a sure fire way to stop herself thinking about the 'what ifs' and 'buts' that seemed to have begun plaguing her mind again. She knew that unless a distraction was found, she would be up all night mulling things over unable to sleep. Her choice had been a good one for it was several hours before any thoughts of calling it a day were given. When eventually she did retire to be comfort of her bed, sleep found her almost straight away.

The following morning Crystal woke to the sound of the alarm clock and hurled a number of expletives at having not altered it with now having no reason to be up so early. She rolled over in an attempt to fall back asleep but it was to no avail. Once she was awake that was it and so she reluctantly threw on some clothes and ventured downstairs to make coffee. With her meeting set for ten o'clock and the time having just past seven, there was that awkward space to fill so as to not arrive too early, but then not get bogged down in something and arrive late. She finished her coffee and returned upstairs to throw herself in the shower, not only could she waste a little time in there, but also by having to dry her hair afterwards. With the time edging towards a more respectable time to leave, Crystal finished getting ready and made her way to the front door. She resisted the urge to think that today may be the start of her happy ever after, especially given the outcome the last time she dared to think that, but there was a good feeling about the day that made her smile.

Another good omen was the fact the train was on time and unlike the night before, there were the occasional seat to be had. Crystal sat and kept telling herself, 'Be confident, be assertive and remember to smile.' The young man who was sitting next to her leaned over to ask, 'Job interview?' She looked at him puzzled for a second before the realisation that he had obviously over heard her. 'No just a meeting with my bank manager.' He smiled returning to his normal sitting position, 'Rather you than me. Give to the rich and be damned the rest of us' he offered whimsically. 'In that case, I hope he considers me rich' she retorted with the same degree of whimsy.

Upon leaving the train Crystal took the short trip through town to her bank. Being slightly earlier than planned, all she could do was wait in the foyer. A young woman arrived and handed her some forms suggesting that filling them in now would save a little time later. 'What's today's date? That would be Wednesday the, wait Wednesday!' She stopped mid thought remembering that today would have been a *meet up with Sean* day. 'I wonder if he would be true to his word.' Until that moment, all thoughts of meeting up with him had been suppressed by the rollercoaster ride she had been on since getting back. Though tinged with a touch of guilt for having forgotten of his promise to visit their meeting place on the same day until she such time that they met again, of course until now, she couldn't help but feel her day getting better and better. Crystal returned to completing the forms praying now that her impending meeting would not be the pin to burst her bubble.

It didn't take too long. Her proposals were well thought out and she sold herself well as someone who could make the most of the opportunity given the chance. Coming away from the meeting her little bubble of happiness was still very much intact, along with ten thousand pound in her account. He definitely deserved the hug rather than the hand shake he offered. Leaving the bank to join the hustle and bustle of folk going about their business, there was no hiding her happiness. Crystal let out a huge cheer that had people turning their heads in her direction. 'Heaven, I'm coming for you.' She screamed looking towards the sky as those looking on shook their heads and went about their business.

Crystal looked at the time, and although her natural urge was to make haste to her favourite bookshop and hand over a cheque to make it hers, that would in all honesty make her late for that possible meet up with Sean. Heaven it seemed would have to wait a little longer as she made her way to their regular meet up place. Being early here also, she would be waiting again. As he had always been then when she arrived from work, hopefully she would not have to wait too long. Crystal ordered a coffee and took a seat at a table close to the door so as to be easily seen when he arrived. She did not have to wait too long as her arrived just as her drink did. 'I'll have one of those too if you'd be so kind' he asked the young woman holding the tray. 'And there was me thinking I would be dinning alone for the next few weeks' he jokingly jibed towards Crystal. She smiled, 'You could say I missed you.' The two sat and drank coffee whilst she started to explain the events of the past week, seven days that seemed like a lifetime.

'So you went to Spain, objected to the plans they had for the place, something I personally commend you for, came back home to quit your job, and now you're about to buy your own business. Wow. Quite the eventful week.' he remarked 'and there was me being proud of finishing the work for the magazine.' Crystal looked with excitement at Sean's news, 'So where and when will I be able to read it? Was it the story set in the brothel? How many parts are there?' He could not help himself smiling at the eagerness at which she asked the questions and answered them to delight her further. 'I'm so pleased for you' she said 'your work is exceptional and deserves an audience.' Sean slumped back in his chair somewhat shying away from the compliments being given. 'Shall we order food?' he asked.

The pair sat for more than an hour in deep conversation and enjoying the food they had chosen. It was Sean that first suggested that he would have to leave soon. 'Here. I thought you may like to read a little more of the original piece I gave to you before I go.' He handed her a small piece of paper which she did indeed begin to read.

It was with great fortune that our paths crossed again. I had given little hope to having seen her once more and yet there she stood before me. My previous assumptions of her being a madam were to be well justified given the manner of which she spoke. No lady would ask of a man his preference in matters that concern sides of a bosom, certainly not in such a public place. I have to say she intrigued me and for lack of my better judgement a further meeting was agreed to later that day. The intent was not for actions that I dare not write, but for learning more of her mind and her life, something we have in common. I can only speak for myself, but a friendship was born of this chance of meetings.

'I find it funny you think of me as a high end prostitute' she said laughingly after finishing the piece. 'But I am really glad, how did you put it? We became friends from a chance meeting.' Sean nervously smiled having no retort to her prostitute comment. 'I'm really glad you came back.' he said standing from his seat, 'but alas I have other places to be and people to meet.' Crystal stood too gathering her belongings. 'Do you have time to come and see where it is I will be buying?' she asked. Sean paused for a second. 'Crystal, I value our friendship very much and it is one that was built around us meeting here on the same day at the same time each week. We spend an hour or so talking about what has happened to each other and that suits me. I have no other friends as they demand too much of my time and the friendship get tied down with trivial matters deemed necessary to share in order to keep the bond alive.' All she could manage was a confused look unsure of just what he was trying to say. 'We know very little about each other outside this moment each week. It serves as a welcome distraction in my week in which I get to meet someone who demands no more of my time than this one moment. Do you understand?' Crystal tried to piece together the key points from all that he had said. 'You just want us to continue as we have been doing?' Sean nodded. 'That's exactly it.'

The two engaged in a hug before going their separate ways once more. She could not help but feel a little disappointed that their friendship would consist of one meeting a week, on a Wednesday during lunch. Though she had to admit there was truth in what he was saying, perhaps he could have offered a little more. It also seemed that no matter how hard she tried, routines were still playing a part in her life. Crystal tried to put her disappointment behind her as she made her way to the bookshop.

As she entered the aroma hit her as it always had. The owner was adding another box of books to the already bulging piles that threatened to make moving around the shop impossible. 'I do hope the valuation hasn't just gone up already' she joked pointing to the new box. 'So you're still thinking of buying then?' he enquired not looking away from the task in hand for fear of sending books everywhere. 'Oh I've finished thinking, and ready to write you a cheque if you're still serious about selling' she offered with a smile. She waited as he finally found the balancing point for the box and turned to face her. 'Really! You seriously wish to part with ten thousand for this place? Come, let us talk business.' The two of them made their way around the maze of bookshelves and piled boxes to the counter to discuss the deal.

It wasn't long before the paperwork was signed and a cheque was signed confirming the change of ownership to Crystal. She was now the proud owner of her very own bookshop and in her eyes, personal library. It was hard to tell who had the biggest smile as the previous owner left immediately waving the cheque and Crystal who set about making plans to make the place her own. The first thing she would need to do was find a way to get paying customers, after all she now had a huge loan to pay each month as well as other bills that would continue to keep coming in. First on the agenda was to return to her old place of work to convince Rupert into giving her a better deal on the lease. If her time in real estate had taught her one thing, it was there was always a deal to be had. With no customers in and no real sign of any imminent, she placed a sign in the window and headed for her old office.

Confidently she walked right in amid shocked faces once more. 'Couldn't stay away from the place eh?' one old colleague jibed. 'Come grovelling to be taken back no doubt' came another. She ignored them all and proceeded to knock on the office door of Mr Hines. She accepted his invitation to *enter* and ignored his comments too about returning to work. Instead she sat opposite him and thrashed out a deal that saw her get a generous reduction on the lease of her new shop. To say he was a little perplexed as to why she had left such a good position in his company to sell tatty old books was an understatement, and he took every chance to let her know his thoughts on her new enterprise. Crystal stood with a deal in place and headed for the door. 'For the first time I'm doing something that makes me happy. I guess that's hard for you to understand Rupert, but there is more to life than making obscene amounts of money.' He looked at her with a blank expression as if the words she had just spoken made no sense at all. 'Goodbye Rupert. I'll see you again when we discuss the renewal' she said with a smile before closing the door behind her. Feeling satisfied with the outcome of their meeting, she confidently made her way out of the office ignoring again all the talk aimed at her by her former colleagues. There was a sense of relief at never having to be the subject for their idle gossip again, but felt for the one their attentions would now turn.

Making her way back to her shop, Crystal decided that the first change she made was to give the place a new name. There was nothing especially bad about the old one, but determined to put her identity on the place she wracked her mind for a new one. Considering everything she had been through recently and what owning this shop symbolised, there was only really one name she could call it, A New Leaf. Sitting in the tatty old chair set aside for reading, Crystal realised the charm of the place was in it quirkiness. It wasn't just a book shop but a sanctuary to all books. It did not need the modern shelving and bright lights of other high street shops, but a careful helping hand in emphasizing its quirky charm.

For the rest of the day Crystal starting upon the monumental task of organising every box in the shop and quickly came to the conclusion that if she was to make any impression on the vast array of books, it was going to take a lot of patience and an organised mind, both were something she was blessed with in abundance as well as a determination to turn this little shop into a haven for book lovers all across town. It was the little piece of heaven she had long been looking for and the best part was she had the paperwork to confirm she owned it.

At the end of the day, Crystal looked around and admired her progress. It may not have been much of an impact, but it was a start to be proud of. Turning the key in the lock and walking away from the shop filled her with more satisfaction than any of the days leaving work from her former office. It felt as though finally everything was falling into place. She caught the train home and made the short walk to her front door. Inside the cosy greeting of warmth from the heating caressed her gently and a smile broke across her face. 'Home sweet home.' Crystal made her way upstairs to change and freshen up before setting about preparing something fresh and tasty for tea. The house was filled with wonderful smells reminiscent of those from Catalina's kitchen. It was another element that helped to make it feel like home. For the rest of evening Crystal indulged in the consuming the fine spread of food she had prepared along with a well-deserved glass wine. 'Well it may have been an unconventional road to happiness, but I think I finally found that elusive slice of heaven.'

In the weeks that passed, Crystal had turned her shop into a quirky old bookshop blending seamlessly the feeling of an old library with modern advertising incorporating social media and internet. Her customer base increased to provide her with a comfortable means of living and although she never did get the designer shoes she promised herself, given the chance she still liked to partake in the occasional window shopping trip. On Wednesday lunchtimes she would meet up with Sean and share in a tales of what they had been up to. It was a friendship as quirky as her shop, but for the two of them it worked beautifully. Every morning Crystal woke on the chimes of seven am and thanked whatever genie it was that was listening to her all those weeks ago for setting her on a journey that ended in her finding exactly what it was she was missing, happiness in every aspect of her life.

The End